"You may kiss the bride," he concluded with a flourish that she felt was wholly unnecessary.

Later, when she was alone, she would quiz herself over why she'd had it in her head that Lukas *wouldn't* kiss her. Why a part of her had felt so ruffled by the idea of him…*declining* to do so. Later.

Not now.

Instead Oti watched, almost transfixed, as he lifted one hand and moved it to her cheek; then he slid it around the back of her neck in a way that any onlooker might have even considered to be romantic. She knew the truth, and yet it almost fooled her.

Then he hauled her to meet him, his eyes burning through her, wild and untamed, and stirring up sensations inside that she was sure she'd never felt before. Then he lowered his head, and as he claimed her mouth with his, her entire body seemed to self-combust in flashes of white-hot heat.

And Oti's world as she knew it imploded.

Dear Reader,

I truly enjoyed writing about Oti and Lukas. I loved learning about them as their story seemed to play out in the best way ever…like a TV script inside my head.

Initially, I feared that Oti was too gentle and overly self-sacrificing, letting her father blackmail her. But every time I put her together with Lukas, she revealed this unexpectedly sassy, fun side, which I think surprised me as much as it unsettled him.

Lukas, by contrast, was so guarded that I think only gentle Oti could have got under this hero's skin the way that she did.

I really hope you enjoy reading Oti and Lukas's story as much as I enjoyed writing it!

I love hearing from my readers, so feel free to drop by my site at www.charlotte-hawkes.com or pop over to Facebook or Twitter, @chawkesuk.

I can't wait to meet you.

Charlotte x

TEMPTED BY HER CONVENIENT HUSBAND

—

CHARLOTTE HAWKES

HARLEQUIN
MEDICAL
ROMANCE

HARLEQUIN®
MEDICAL
ROMANCE™

Recycling programs
for this product may
not exist in your area.

ISBN-13: 978-1-335-40880-8

Tempted by Her Convenient Husband

Copyright © 2021 by Charlotte Hawkes

This edition published by arrangement with Harlequin Books S.A.

For questions and comments about the quality of this book,
please contact us at CustomerService@Harlequin.com.

Harlequin Enterprises ULC
22 Adelaide St. West, 40th Floor
Toronto, Ontario M5H 4E3, Canada
www.Harlequin.com

Printed in U.S.A.

Born and raised on the Wirral Peninsula in England, **Charlotte Hawkes** is mom to two intrepid boys who love her to play building block games with them and who object loudly to the amount of time she spends on the computer. When she isn't writing—or building with blocks—she is company director for a small Anglo/French construction firm. Charlotte loves to hear from readers, and you can contact her at her website, charlotte-hawkes.com.

Books by Charlotte Hawkes

Harlequin Medical Romance

The Island Clinic

Reunited with His Long-Lost Nurse

Royal Christmas at Seattle General

The Bodyguard's Christmas Proposal

Reunited on the Front Line

Second Chance with His Army Doc
Reawakened by Her Army Major

A Summer in São Paolo

Falling for the Single Dad Surgeon

Unwrapping the Neurosurgeon's Heart
Surprise Baby for the Billionaire
The Doctor's One Night to Remember

Visit the Author Profile page at Harlequin.com.

To Vic.

Happy birthday to the newest little wolf
in your fearless pack! X

CHAPTER ONE

'How long has the kid been on the oxytocin drip, Oti?'

'Two hours,' Octavia Hendlington murmured softly. 'Six drops per minute.'

Not turning around as her colleague joined her, Oti continued to eye the young woman perched uncomfortably on the end of the bed and being cared for by her sister. The labour ward—or what passed for the labour ward in this end of the large hospital tent in her medical camp in South Sudan—was tiny.

But they had worked so many miracles in this place over the past four years, she could only hope tonight—her last night—would be a good one.

'Dilation?' Amelia queried.

'She's been at six centimetres for the past ten hours. Her name is Kahsha; she's eighteen, primigravida.'

'And the baby's head still shows no sign of descending?' Amelia frowned.

Oti's teeth worried at her lower lip, and she stopped herself abruptly. In a matter of days she would be back in the UK, and her father would not accept such unattractive, *unladylike* habits.

Five more days of being herself, and then she would be back to playing a role again.

Would her new husband be just as irritated by her as her father had always been? Oti shoved the thought from her head and focused on her colleague.

'No sign of the baby descending at all,' she told Amelia.

She cast her gaze around the tent and tried to swallow down the thick lump of emotion that lodged itself so uncomfortably in her throat. If it hadn't been for the fact that it looked as if it was going to be a complicated labour, Oti might have been grateful for the distraction from her own thoughts tonight.

She had been volunteering with the medical charity HOP—Health Overseas Project—for four years, ever since her brother's accident, and this was the only place where she'd ever felt herself. Possibly the only time in her life—certainly in the last fifteen years.

Dr Oti.

It was simple and clean, and she thought that was perhaps what she loved the most. Out here, far away from the clamour of home, it was just about helping people and making a difference.

She had value.

Surely that was as uncomplicated as it got?

But soon that would all be over. And it didn't matter which mask she would be donning this time—Oti the socialite, the It-girl, or Lady Octavia Hendlington, daughter of the Earl of Sedeshire and soon-to-be Lady Octavia Woods— it would still suffocate her, just the same.

What would Amelia and the other volunteers think if they knew she was about to marry the much-lusted-after billionaire, Lukas Woods? Or *Sir* Lukas Woods—given the knighthood he had received in the previous year's New Year's Honours list. Not the youngest recipient, but certainly one of the youngest.

Busying herself with the oxytocin drip, as though occupying her hands could also occupy her wayward mind, Oti tried to pretend that her stomach hadn't just flip-flopped at the thought.

The man was one of the most eligible bachelors in the world right now—certainly one of the most eligible in the country—and in five days she would be marrying him. The thought was terrifying.

Lukas Woods wasn't merely good-looking… he was practically elemental. As though there was fire, earth, wind and water…and then there was *him*. And that beautifully muscled exterior was rivalled only by his inner core of pure steel. Ruthless business magnate, media personality and self-made billionaire. How many other kids had written an app at the age of fifteen, and made their first million by the age of eighteen?

She might have met him on only that one intimidating occasion five months earlier, but it had been enough to leave her with the impression that he might as well have been honed from the very magma of the planet itself.

How was she ever to endure a marriage to this man? This stranger? What if she couldn't even stand him?

Her body prickled in protest, and she ignored the tiny voice inside taunting her that she already knew the answer to that question.

Then again, the alternative had been a forced marriage to Louis Rockman, son of the Sixth Earl of Highmount, vicious, dictatorial and cruel. Even now, fifteen years on, she could still feel the grip of his fingers biting into her arms, his weight pinning her down...

'You're thinking a C-section?'

Amelia's voice dragged her mercifully back to the present.

'Yes. But now Kahsha wants to return to her own village to seek out help from a traditional healer.'

'Right.' Amelia nodded grimly. 'It's her choice, Oti.'

Oti dipped her head. They both knew that they couldn't stop the young girl from seeking traditional help if that was what she chose to do. HOP had long drilled it into their volunteers that they were there to offer medical advice and options, but not dictate. Some of the women they encountered had little enough autonomy over their own lives as it was. They didn't need a group of foreigners swooping in and taking away their choices on how they wanted to give birth.

It was enough that the charity's volunteers showed respect for the decisions the Sudanese women made about their own deliveries and their own health.

'It just doesn't help when it isn't what's medically best for them.' Oti folded her arms over her chest, making her friend frown at her.

'You okay? I've never seen you quite this on edge.'

Oti had no idea how she managed to summon what she hoped was a bright smile.

'Of course. Just tired probably. It's been another twenty-hour shift.'

Her colleague looked unconvinced, and Oti knew why. Shifts were always long in a camp like this, but she'd never been this down. Perhaps a version of the truth would be better. She tried ramping the smile up a little more.

'I'm think I'm going to miss this place.'

'I'm so sorry.' Amelia grimaced, understanding washing over her expression. 'I forgot you were leaving tomorrow. But you'll be back in a few months, right? You always are. What is it now, forty months out of the past four years that you've been out here?'

'Something like that.' Oti forced a laugh, as though she was any normal person looking forward to spending some time back home again. Ironically, another role that she knew how to play.

She hadn't told anyone that this would be her last mission, any more than she'd told them that she was getting married. It would only invite too many questions that she wouldn't know how to answer.

Or perhaps it was more that saying it aloud would somehow make it too real.

'Go and get something to eat, and get your head down,' her colleague advised. 'You've got a five-hour drive just to the nearest airstrip.'

'Sure.' It felt more like an awkward jerk of her head than a nod, but at least Amelia didn't seem to notice anything amiss.

She felt foolish. But what choice did she have, either about telling her colleagues, or about agreeing to the marriage in the first instance?

You could have said no, a voice whispered in her head, but Oti shut it down quickly.

True, Lukas Woods had asked her if she was sure she knew what she was doing, but declining him had never been a real option. Not if she wanted to save her brother. Her father had made that abundantly clear.

Her father hadn't earned the title The Odious Earl for nothing, even if no one dared say it to his face. Not even her.

Especially not her.

Shaking her head free of the dark thoughts that threatened to overtake her, Oti watched the young mum-to-be struggle off the bed with the help of her sister and managed another smile at her colleague.

'I think I might accompany Kahsha just a short way out of camp. You never know, the walking might help the baby to descend and we won't need to try for a C-section after all.'

It was always possible. And, anyway, if this was to be her last trip out to Sub-Saharan Africa for a while—or ever—then she might as well absorb every last second of it.

Because all she saw for her future were even more fences to hem her in than she'd ever had to endure before.

As the organist played a virtuosic performance of Bizet's 'Farandole,' Lukas watched his bride being led up the aisle by her father. Though *led* might be too mild a word for it, given that the man could evidently barely restrain himself. The Odious Earl—a nickname that the man had earned for his pomposity, his gambling and his penchant for young girls barely older than his own daughter—was practically racing to deliver Lady Octavia to her fate.

Not that Lukas cared to look too closely, but he was sure that if he did he would actually be able to see pound signs imprinted in the Earl's eyes, the older man's podgy fingers virtually grasping for the hefty sum of money that would be his on conclusion of the ceremony.

Involuntarily, Lukas's gaze shifted to the taller than average, slightly willowy figure walking beside him with no fewer than seven bridesmaids in tow, although she eclipsed every one of them. An observation which he chose to ignore—along with the inconvenient and somewhat galling way that his body tightened in response.

This marriage wasn't about love, or even lust. It was about securing the controlling interest in Octavia's late brother's company, Sedeshire International, as the latest acquisition for Lukas's own company, LVW Industries. Preferably before the idiot Earl ran his late son's company into the ground, as he had been doing in the short time that he'd had his hands on it.

And if marrying the old Earl's socialite daughter was the price he had to pay for it—along with an eye-watering sum, of course—then Lukas considered it money well spent.

The business was actually a good investment, but the fact that he'd stolen it from right under the nose of Andrew Rockman, the Sixth Earl of Highmount, had been a delicious bonus.

How fitting that this was how Lukas would finally be able to fulfil the vow he had made to himself as a twelve-year-old, the week his mother had been lowered into that black hole in the ground—that he would one day take his revenge on the Rockman family. In particular that he would take his revenge on Rockman, the man who had effectively driven her there, along with Lady Octavia's father, the man who had helped Rockman get away with his lies.

And, by marrying him, Lady Octavia would unwittingly help him to bring her repugnant father into line.

Yet as Lukas watched their approach closely, he was sure he saw her wobble. The faintest stumble before her father lowered his head to hers and murmured something that looked tender but which Lukas imagined was anything but. His bride-to-be seemed to stiffen her resolve even as a beatific smile graced her full mouth, and her eyes flickered up to meet Lukas's own.

And something slammed into him.

Just as it had five months ago, when he'd visited Sedeshire Hall to ensure that she knew and agreed to the marriage, only for Lady Octavia to walk—no, *stride*—into that conservatory at her family home, carrying herself like a queen rather than a mere *lady*. She'd made his entire body leap on sight, even as she'd declared confidently that, deal or not, she knew what she was doing and she was prepared to marry him.

As though the decision had been hers.

Desire had walloped him then, just as it did now. Hard. Like a punch to the gut when a fighter dropped his guard in a bout—which he *never* did. He'd wanted her right there and then. Like nothing he'd ever known before.

And then she'd fixed him with that inscrutable stare of hers—with eyes far too intelligent and fierce and assessing than the air-headed, social-climbing creature he'd been led to believe she was.

Making him wonder at the veracity of all those rumours. Making him wonder if she really was such a vacuous socialite and making him want to piece together the fascinating puzzle that this woman suggested she was.

And that killer body that she seemed to have absolutely no idea that she possessed.

He'd known she was pretty enough. The photos of her exploits as an It-girl—clad in scraps of metallic dress or barely-there bikinis—revealed as much, though he'd believed that her personality would be as plasticky as so many socialites of his acquaintance. Perhaps that explained why he hadn't been prepared for the almost visceral reaction he'd had to her.

In that one moment, five months ago, he'd been

taken over by a desire that he'd never experienced before in his life. He had never wanted a woman so badly, with such a *need* that he thought he might go mad if he didn't have her.

And yet at the same time, crazily, he'd wanted to protect her. From her father. And maybe from others. Perhaps that was the part of it which made the least sense.

He'd wanted to throw her over his shoulder and carry her out of that place, and if he'd had a damned horse then he'd believed he might have thrown her over that too. Rescuing her as if he was some medieval knight instead of a modern-day one, and she was his damsel in distress.

He, who had never been given to flights of fantasy in all his years.

It was the moment Lukas had realised that Lady Octavia Hendlington was the last woman on earth he should ever marry. Yet he'd done nothing to stop it, and now this vision was gliding gracefully up the aisle towards him, and she was no pretty-but-plastic girl. She appeared every inch a stunning woman with an indefinable quality that Lukas could neither put his finger on nor dismiss.

It unsettled him.

Not for the first time, he felt the tiptoeing steps of doubt creep into his brain, casting the faintest black shadow.

And, not for the first time, Lukas shut it out.

So she was attractive. It meant nothing that he noticed—he was, after all, a red-blooded male—but it didn't mean he couldn't control it, this jolt of heat that she seemed capable of igniting within him.

Attraction was fleeting; flames died. And, no matter how innocent his bride-to-be appeared on the outside, he could not afford to forget that Lady Octavia Hendlington was an autumn crocus—beautiful to look at and seemingly harmless, but in reality she was toxic right through. Just like her father.

Finally, she drew to an elegant halt beside him and he was suddenly struck once again by quite how vivid, how piercing her eyes were. A blue that almost seemed to reach inside him and strike that black thing which had long since resided where a heart would normally be.

He couldn't bring himself to look away. Worse, he didn't want to.

So as she stood before him, calmly allowing her bridesmaids to sort out the ridiculously long train of her wedding gown, Lukas fought to rein himself in, telling himself that the interlude was also a chance to get a grip on his own traitorous reactions.

'You made it then,' he remarked drily. For her ears only. As though engaging in banal conversation could somehow lessen her impact on him.

But, as she tilted her head up to him even further, that punch became a fist, tightening around his lower gut. He forced himself to ignore it.

'Did you think I wouldn't?' she asked.

'It crossed my mind. Especially since your father told me that you were at your *special* spa retreat, which I understand is your social circle's euphemism for *rehab*. Again.'

'I wasn't in rehab,' she bit out, and he couldn't have said why he thought she hadn't intended to speak.

For a moment it appeared that she was going to say something else, but then she blinked at him and closed her mouth. The air seemed to shift around them, leaving Lukas uncharacteristically unsettled. As though he'd somehow missed the mark.

But he hadn't. It had been well-documented in the media that the first time she'd attended some kind of rehab she'd been fifteen, about the time her out-of-control partying had really begun to hit the headlines. Although she'd been decidedly more discreet in the past decade or so, the rumours had persisted.

That was presumably why her father had insisted on Lukas marrying her as part of the deal for Sedeshire International.

Without warning, his bride-to-be turned her head elegantly to look around the cathedral.

'Verging on overkill, don't you think?'

He followed her eyes as she glanced around.

Bedecked in flowers, with the bells pealing and the world-renowned organist still playing, it was acutely apparent that no expense had been spared. Ordered—though none of it paid for— by her father, of course.

Luxurious wreaths and wide velvet ribbons hung from the magnificent, towering stone columns, while generous bouquets of calla lilies and baby's breath decorated each and every pew filled with the four hundred or so guests.

'Precisely how I believe you instructed it,' Lukas replied drily.

Or perhaps, more likely, as had been instructed by some young twenty-something would-be party planner, and the Earl's latest badly kept secret.

If he hadn't known better, he might have thought his bride-to-be actually winced. But if she did, she caught herself quickly.

'Of course. And the fitted lace gown, a six-foot-long train and thirty silk buttons complete with rouleau loops?' she bit out.

'It's from the most sought-after designer of the moment—just as I believe you requested.'

'Really? You believe I requested a wedding gown so tight that I had to pour myself into it and then be sewn in place?' She couldn't help herself; her discreet tone did nothing to disguise the barbed note to her words. 'It leaves nothing to the imagination.'

The organist was concluding now and the

bishop was preparing to deliver his address, so Lukas had to move his head even closer to her ear to ensure they weren't heard.

Instantly he became aware that her scent—fresh and light, and not remotely cloying—was assailing his senses.

Making his body tighten all the more.

'If you'd wanted a say in the design of your wedding dress, and if you weren't in rehab, *Lady* Octavia...' he didn't know why he felt the need to emphasise her name just then—perhaps to keep his mind on the game? '...then perhaps you should have bothered to come back and deal with it, rather than spending the last few months partying and sunning yourself on one beach after the next.'

She glowered. 'Are you guessing now?'

'I don't need to. Your glowing tan rather gives it away,' he made himself say. 'But, either way, does it matter?'

There was the briefest of pauses, as though she wanted to say something—perhaps along the lines that it mattered to her. But instead she flashed a bright smile which he couldn't help feeling was a little too practised.

'Of course not.' Her smile had an edge that felt an awful lot like a blade. 'I've long held the title of Sedeshire's lost cause heiress, after all.'

'Then all the more reason to make it a show and quell any rumours that this is some hastily arranged marriage simply because you are pregnant with my—or any other man's—child.'

She bristled, though he suspected he was the only one close enough to spot it.

'Does that title concern you?' he couldn't help himself from asking.

'Lost cause heiress?' Her head snapped up. 'Of course not. I learned years ago not to care what anyone thought.'

He couldn't have said why, but he didn't entirely believe her.

'And, for what it's worth, the lace alone on your bridesmaids' gowns took months to sew,' Lukas added, 'so there will be no question that this wedding took care, and planning, and time. I hope you enjoyed those last months of heady indulgence. But I should warn you, your partying lifestyle is now at an end.'

'How very autocratic of you,' she bit out before she could stop herself. 'And between the intricate lace of my bridesmaids' dresses and the tightness of this one to show that there is no baby bump concealed beneath, I'm flattered that you paid such close attention.'

'As you should be.'

Before she could work out whether he was serious or still mocking, he flashed her a wolfish smile.

'Perhaps, though, having you as the mother of

my heir could be a wise selection. Good stock, as they say.'

He knew he would score a hit even before he said the words. There had never been any mention of heirs before, even if he couldn't entirely explain what had made him even say it.

It seemed his bride-to-be got under his skin a little too much, but she didn't need to know that. Neither did she need to know that he was lying about heirs; he had never had any intention of ever perpetuating his cold, damaged bloodline.

Not with a father—biologically, if nothing else—like his.

Still, something in Lukas had uttered the words, and now he relished the way his soon-to-be-bride practically bubbled with indignation.

And something else he chose not to identify.

CHAPTER TWO

HE COULD NOT be serious?

Oti bristled as his eyes raked over her and pretended that he didn't leave a scorching trail of awareness right from the top of her head to the tips of her toes. And everything in between.

Especially everything in between.

'And should I present my head for inspection so that you can ensure there are no bulges or depressions which may indicate any dental issues?' she sniped, her voice just on the brink of being loud enough to be overheard, before she caught herself. 'Perhaps you'd care to examine my legs to ensure they're symmetrical and well balanced, and that there is no sensitivity or similar problem to the structure?'

'I'll presume that's how you inspect a horse or some such animal, shall I?' His low voice seemed to ripple the air in the space between them. 'How clichéd that someone with your upbringing should use that as a frame of reference.'

'And how banal that a self-made man from one

of the worst estates in the country would look down on me for doing so,' she shot back acerbically, though she made sure the smile never slipped from her lips.

'Touché,' he acknowledged instead. 'It seems we each continue to prejudge the other.'

'Although, in my case, I believe my judgement is rather more accurate, is it not?'

Even as she said it, she couldn't stop herself from shivering at the way every single person was watching her. Prejudging her in exactly the way that Lukas was talking about.

Weighing her up. Measuring her. Damning her.

All of them wanting to know what she'd done to land the much-chased infamous playboy and marriage-phobic Lukas Woods.

He'd been right about the dress—as galling as that was—half of them probably thought she was already pregnant. Deliberately.

'Smile,' he instructed brusquely, offering a flash of straight white teeth that any onlooker might believe was a genuine smile.

And Oti obeyed, ignoring the way her heart was pounding in her chest—assuring her that her adrenaline was all fired up and ready to carry her at speed, straight back out and to the waiting car.

But she couldn't. Not just because of her father, whose grip on her arm had been so tight as he'd propelled her down the aisle that she could still feel the bruise forming under her skin even now. Not just because she couldn't bring herself to humiliate Lukas like that, when, despite everything, he had at least given her a chance—two chances—to back out of this marriage. But because she had no idea where that would leave Edward.

Edward—how could she leave him to their father? Her heart had practically broken the last time she'd visited and he'd begged her to help him end it all with dignity, only to threaten to ban her from visiting again when she'd refused.

'Octavia? What is it?'

She tried to speak but choked on the words, yet the bishop droned on, oblivious, mercifully too caught up in his own self-important role to notice.

'Did he hurt you?'

She blinked, taking a moment to realise that she was massaging the tender spot on her arm. She dropped her hand instantly. Lukas already looked furious, as though he was just looking for an excuse to call the wedding off.

She couldn't blame him; marrying Lukas, taking his money, was all a lie. But it would give her a chance to help save Edward's life, so how could she refuse?

'Of course he didn't hurt me,' she lied smoothly. But she couldn't help adding, 'After all, my father *is* an honourable man.'

She hadn't expected Lukas to get the reference, but he arched an eyebrow almost imperceptibly.

'Marc Antony?' his voice rumbled. 'His oration at Julius Caesar's funeral.'

It was a long-standing joke between her and Edward. She certainly hadn't expected Lukas Woods to get it. She blinked quickly.

'Yes.'

'Interesting,' he murmured, his eyes holding hers.

Rare, dark granite-grey with perhaps the faintest hint of a midnight blue flecked through them. And they rooted her to the mosaic floor.

'If you see yourself as some kind of Marc Antony, and your father as Brutus, then who might you cast in the role of Cassius, I wonder? Or even Caesar himself?'

Wordlessly, Oti stared at him.

If she'd hoped that her months away would diminish the effect he had on her—even during their one single meeting, five months ago in the conservatory of Sedeshire Hall—then Oti now realised she'd been wholly naïve.

'I keep looking at you and thinking you present yourself as quite the incapable, guileless young woman in this entire agreement. But you aren't, are you?'

She blinked. It was true that she wasn't herself around Lukas. She hadn't been even from that first moment.

For a woman who had always prided herself on her gentle nature and giving personality, she seemed to turn into this smart-mouthed sass machine whenever Lukas Woods was near. It would have been disconcerting if she hadn't decided it was a good defence mechanism. And she was only with him for Edward's sake. Not her own.

'Perhaps we should try needling each other a little less?' he suggested as the bishop began to wrap up his opening speech. 'Given that we're about to become husband and wife.'

Husband and wife.

Oti knew it had been meant as a light quip, but the words echoed through her head as a strange sensation poured through her. And this time it had nothing to do with the low, impossibly rich voice that coiled around her unexpectedly, seeming to permeate her very bones and making her feel...*odd.* Or the way his mouth was so close to her ear that his warming breath brought jolts of unwanted attraction straight down her centre. To her core.

Husband and wife, it echoed again.

And she tried to pretend that something didn't kick hard in her chest. Or lower, if she were to be shamefully honest.

What was she thinking, taking on a man like this...marrying him?

Even for her brother. But what choice had she had? She could finally see the light at the end of the proverbial tunnel, when the last four years had pitched them all into the blackness. How could she have done anything but run towards it and hope that it was the way out, and not another oncoming train?

It was odd, wasn't it? The way her life seemed to be cleaved into such clear segments. It was as if she'd been reeling from one thing to another— her attack, her mother's death, then Edward's accident—these past fifteen years. Reacting. Countering. Hopelessly out of control. But always playing catch-up.

She hadn't had time to breathe or think. Or even work out the person she was.

She'd thought she'd been getting closer to finding herself these last years with HOP. Working in South Sudan had been the first thing that had truly felt her own. It had helped to ground her. At least her last memory out there was of the walk with the young mum Kahsha, where the prolonged exercise had finally helped the baby to shift and descend.

Now there was a five-day-old baby back near their camp called Ayshani-Oti. Her heart actually felt as though it was going to swell its way out of her chest.

If only her father's Machiavellian wrangling hadn't once again caught up with her. He started fires wherever he went. Destroyed everything. He'd used Edward against her, and she'd had no choice but to fling herself once more into a burning building in the hope that she could put the fire out.

Only this time the fire was Lukas Woods. And she couldn't help fearing that he was going to be the one to finally burn her.

'If any person present knows of any lawful impediment to this marriage, speak now or for ever hold your peace.'

Oti tuned back in as the bishop was speaking, the silence descending in the cathedral seeming suddenly so loud in her ears. The vaulted ceilings echoed with the sound of a guest coughing. Someone sneezing. And all she could think was that she had a hundred objections to going through with the marriage.

Not least the fact that she no longer trusted herself or her motives. Not entirely.

And then she caught Lukas's grim expression and she couldn't have said what that sensation was that rolled through her; it was as though he was waiting for someone to object. But no one did.

Another cough.

Another shuffle of bottom against wooden pew.

And Lukas merely watched her. Challenging her. And taunting her. Baring his teeth in something that might appear to be a smile but made Oti think of wolves and sharpened fangs.

She needed to keep her head in the game, lest

she end up being ripped to shreds. And she could pretend to be offended by the entire agreement all she liked—she certainly ought to be—but the truth was that she was floored by her insane attraction to Lukas.

She had been, right from the moment she'd walked into that room in Sedeshire Hall five months ago. He'd made every reservation she had about the ludicrous marriage disappear from her brain.

Or maybe it was more that her brain had ceased working altogether.

Despite all the pictures she'd ever seen of him in the papers—and there was a plethora of them, all displaying the man in all his honed magnificence—not one of them had even come close to conveying quite how *breathtaking* he was up close.

Quite how *heart-stopping.*

Six feet and four inches of pure, sizzling muscle that—she'd realised after a startling instant—had her hands actually itching to reach out and touch. To see if, beneath that exquisitely tailored suit that had clung so lovingly to his broad shoulders, he could possibly be as rock-solid as he looked. As though he was magnificent enough to rival even the most famous of the Greek statues. Myron's *Discobolus*, perhaps. Or Glykon's *Farnese Herakles.*

Oti had always considered herself relatively

cultured, interested in such works of art on a purely intellectual level. *Up until that moment.* But, standing there in that room, it had been as though her whole world had suddenly tipped up on end and shifted. She'd felt more and more pyretic the longer she'd been in Lukas's company and though she'd pretended it was just the circumstances of their meeting, she'd known it had all been a lie.

Now, there was no lying any more.

The bishop smiled benevolently at them and declared his delight at leading the marriage vows.

Oti's heart gave another lurch.

'And so it begins,' Lukas murmured as he shot her a smile that, to the congregation, would surely have looked like a smile between lovers.

But she knew better. She was close enough to see the expression in those hard grey eyes. And the smile wasn't reflected in them at all. Her heart began to hammer.

It hammered so loudly, in fact, that she could scarcely hear anything else for the rest of the service. Not the bishop's loquacious additions, nor Lukas as he recited his vows, and not even herself as she echoed them.

It was like being in a fog, somewhere in the middle of the hedge maze that used to dominate the west part of the gardens of the Sedeshire estate when her mother had been alive.

As though the entire ceremony was happening to someone else on the other side of the eight-foot evergreens. She could see them but she could barely even hear them.

She would have been happy to stay like that for ever.

Lost.

It was only as the bishop was declaring them husband and wife that Oti finally began to come back to herself.

'You may kiss the bride,' he concluded with a flourish that she felt was wholly unnecessary.

Later, when she was alone, she would quiz herself over why she'd had it in her head that Lukas *wouldn't* kiss her. Why a part of her had felt so ruffled by the idea of him…*declining* to do so. Later.

Not now.

Instead, Oti watched, almost transfixed, as he lifted one hand and moved it to her cheek; then he slid it around the back of her neck in a way that any onlooker might have even considered to be romantic. She knew the truth, and yet it almost fooled her.

Then he hauled her towards him, his eyes burning through her, wild and untamed and stirring up sensations inside that she was sure she'd never felt before. Then he lowered his head and, as he claimed her mouth with his, her entire body seemed to combust in flashes of white-hot heat.

And Oti's world as she knew it imploded.

* * *

He should never have kissed her, Lukas casti-gated himself a short while later when he had finally ushered his too-lovely new bride into the back seat of their wedding car, barking out a low command to his driver before climbing in after her.

He should never have married her either. But that was hard to remember when he was still floored by their kiss. And it didn't help that she was touching her fingers to her lips, with that same dazed expression shining in her too-blue eyes. He tried to pull his gaze away and look out of the window, but it was impossible.

Slowly, she turned her head to look at him. Her throat worked a few times.

'What...was that?'

'If I have to tell you—' his voice was sharp, and not at all like himself '—then I can't have been doing it right. And we both know that isn't the case.'

It spoke volumes that she didn't respond to that with one of her witty put-downs. As if she was too punch-drunk to manage it. Any other time, he might have taken that as a triumph.

But, right now, Lukas was still trying to ration-alise what had happened back in the cathedral. He'd intended a kiss which would satisfy their critics without being inappropriate, but then he'd felt the soft fullness of her mouth open up under his, and everything…*everything* had fallen away.

The cathedral, the guests, even the damned plan itself.

In that split second there had been only him and her. And something that felt oddly like a truth between them.

Which meant that he really was in trouble.

Merely being tempted by the woman was one thing. But it was quite another to forget that anything else even existed. Worse, that he didn't care, because he could still taste her on his tongue. And he found himself savouring it.

Muttering a curse under his breath, he reached towards the limousine's minibar and selected a tumbler before pouring himself a few generous fingers of whisky.

Yeah, he'd realised the kiss had been a mistake even as her breath was heating his mouth back there in the cathedral. He'd tried telling himself that he'd had no choice, that the kiss was an integral part of the ceremony, that he was playing the part of the newly married husband.

But it hadn't felt like playing a part when his mouth had been sliding so perfectly over hers, as though he'd been waiting for this very moment ever since their first encounter. As though *she* was the reason he'd been feeling so edgy for the better part of the last five months, rather than the fact that the plan he had set in motion more than two decades earlier was finally drawing closer.

Close enough to smell.

The first step had been buying out Sedeshire International before the Rockman family could get hold of it, and now those papers were finally signed off and the ink was almost dry. Lukas didn't care that he'd paid over the odds to do so. It was only money and these days he had more of it than his dirt-poor childhood self could ever have even imagined.

The second step was, admittedly, a little harder to swallow, especially for a self-confirmed bachelor—marrying Lady Octavia on the dubious promise that her father would finally tell the truth and set the record straight about his mother.

Just as he had vowed to her as a twelve-year-old.

And it didn't matter that she was no longer around to see justice done, to see her tarnished reputation finally being restored. It would be enough that he had kept his promise to her.

He'd watched the expression of old Andrew Rockman in that front pew, practically incandescent with rage at the marriage.

Lukas had half expected Rockman to storm to the front when the bishop had asked if there were any objections—maybe he would have even welcomed it. The barbaric man would at least have had to finally show his true colours, and the charade would have been over.

But, of course, the opportunity had passed. Rockman had swallowed the rage that only Lukas himself had noticed, and the service had continued. And he'd felt as if he was on autopilot right up to the moment where the slick brush of his lips over Octavia's had made Lukas forget where he was. *Who* he was.

Heat had poured through him as his new bride had melted against him. Right into him. And oh, how there had been a part of him that had craved exactly that.

Lukas couldn't understand it.

Taking a long pull of the expensive drink, he let the heat pour though him and soothe him. But, strangely, he didn't really taste it.

He could only taste *her*. Roaring through his veins, thundering around his being. Flooding him. He could barely restrain himself from reaching over to haul her back to him and explore that delicious friction between them all over again.

His only consolation was that she wanted him just as badly. He knew women well enough to be able to read his new bride like an open book.

Tension emanated off her as she sat across the luxurious seats from him. He could see that she too fought to get herself back under control, the taut lines of her elegant neck at odds with the way she kept her hands neatly folded in her lap, too neat, too precise. As if she could read every last traitorous thought in his head and felt every one of them.

He needed to break the silence, but no words came.

'Drink?' he offered at last, more for something to say. 'Or perhaps that would undermine whatever programme you're following.'

'You mean like a twelve-step one?' She sniffed. 'No, thank you. Though, as I said, I wasn't in rehab. It's just that it's barely eleven thirty.'

Her attempt at a put-down might have amused him under any other circumstances. It certainly wouldn't have got to him. What was wrong with him?

'Says the woman who is well known for partying 24/7,' he countered instead. 'It's a bit late to start pretending to have standards, isn't it?'

'Evidently,' she shot back, though her tone was ridiculously polite. 'Since I just married you. Or perhaps I'm lying and it's the booze and drugs talking.'

He gave a snort of laughter despite himself. Her comebacks were like a fine blade slicing through the air, neither dull nor confused.

Without knowing what he was doing, Lukas stretched one long arm out across the seats. He took her chin in his fingers and—not unkindly— forced her to look at him.

'That's twice you've seemed offended when

I've mentioned your past. But your pupils aren't dilated, and you don't sound compromised. You certainly don't smell like you're drunk. For that matter, you didn't seem under the influence when last we met either. One might actually suspect that the rumours about you weren't wholly true.'

Octavia froze. Her glorious sapphire eyes—which he hated himself for noticing, let alone being unable to draw his gaze away from—widened. Her breathing grew more rapid and shallow. He could see her pulse battering wildly in her neck, the beat seeming to echo throughout his entire body.

It shouldn't have been so hard to make his hand open up. To release her.

Belatedly, his new bride wrenched her head away as if she'd been just as frozen as he had been. If he wasn't careful he could end up blowing this whole scheme on a woman who seemed to be capable of doing the one thing that only one person had ever managed.

It seemed that his new bride was developing a knack for getting under his skin.

The sooner they got this wedding breakfast over with and he could get back to the relative peace of his home—and, more important, his office—the better.

CHAPTER THREE

OTI WAS RELIEVED when their car finally drew up at the reception venue.

She'd spent the entire journey replaying their discussion in church as though they'd been two naughty school children in Sunday service, instead of bride and groom at their own wedding.

It was ludicrous.

Yet even now, thinking of doing...*intimate things* with this man only made her feel all the more edgy. Hotter. And heavier. Right *there*... between her legs.

What was wrong with her?

She couldn't imagine what he would say if he knew the truth. If Lukas found out that she was a virgin. It was embarrassing, certainly at her age. He wouldn't believe her, anyway. Not unless she explained why she'd barely done more than kiss a man in the past decade. Not unless she told him the whole story. And there was no chance she would do that.

She'd put that part of her life—that awful night—behind her a long time ago.

If her brother hadn't come along exactly when he had…well, she didn't like to think what might have—*would* have—happened. It sickened her enough that it had got as far as it had. But she'd been lucky. Edward had rescued her. Too many other women weren't so fortunate.

But Lukas Woods didn't need to know any of it.

Still, as he slid far too gracefully out of the car and then turned to help her follow, she almost batted his hand away, only spotting her bridesmaids—girls she barely knew any more, let alone friends—waiting for her. Every one of them was her father's choice. Mostly daughters of high-ranking nobility with whom he was trying to ingratiate himself. Perhaps one of them was the girl that he was currently sleeping with—though she was barely older than Oti, and possibly a little younger.

Odious didn't quite cover it. If it wasn't for Edward, she would have cut her father out of her life years ago.

Perhaps she would be able to visit her brother soon. Maybe even in the next few days. There was no honeymoon planned; to be fair, she felt as if she was going to be more of a mistress than a wife, since Lukas was already married to his work.

But, for now, she still had the wedding breakfast to get through. Shoving her thoughts to the back of her mind, Oti feigned another smile—her cheeks were beginning to ache—and allowed Lukas to take her hand and assist her out of the vintage vehicle and tried not to wince.

She might have known the infamously sharp-eyed Lukas wouldn't miss it.

'What is it?' He stopped instantly.

'It's nothing,' she lied, trying to turn her arm so that he couldn't see.

Taking her arm and stilling her movements, he noted the bruise that was already beginning to form.

'Was this your father?' he demanded. 'Before, in the cathedral? What was it that he said to you?'

'It's fine. Let's just go inside.'

Not a rebuttal, she noted. As if she wanted Lukas to know.

She eyed the marks, practically feeling her father's vice-like grip as it had tightened around her. His fingers biting painfully into her arm.

'Don't mess this up, girl,' he'd hissed. 'Or, so help you, you and that vegetable brother of yours will regret it.'

Anger had shot through her and she remembered jerking her head up and forcing herself to take one step then another, until finally she drew to an elegant halt at the top of the aisle, where her father finally released her.

If she was going to bolt, *that* had been her chance.

Instead, she'd looked at Lukas and all her fears, all her anger, had seemed to simply...dissolve. As though it was all going to be okay.

Which was why, right now, she just wanted to forget her father and return to whatever verbal jousting she and Lukas had discovered back in the cathedral. As absurd as it was, she'd found some degree of comfort in their barbed exchanges.

'I can't help but notice the inordinate number of devastated-looking Z-list actresses dressed as though they're in mourning,' she murmured as they strode into the magnificent venue.

His jaw locked, and she silently prayed that he wasn't going to continue interrogating her about her father.

'What can I say?' Relenting unexpectedly, Lukas apparently decided to play along. 'I'm quite the catch.'

'It might have been amusing to watch, had I been in the congregation watching that car crash of a wedding, instead of standing right there at the front—one of the main participants.'

'You didn't enjoy being the centre of attention, Octavia? You do surprise me.'

'And then there was Andrew, looking apoplectic.' She snorted indelicately, a fraction of a second before she realised Lukas had stiffened slightly beside her.

'Andrew?' He sounded as though he could barely bring himself to spit the word out.

Oti frowned. 'Andrew Rockman, Sixth Earl of Highmount?' she clarified. 'He and my father are as thick as thieves, which should tell you everything you need to know about the man.'

'I know who he is.' The clipped tone made her stomach flip.

'You're not friends?' She didn't know if she could stand that.

'We are most certainly not.'

She was pretty sure that the unrufflable Lukas Woods was seething beneath his too-flattering morning suit.

How curious.

'Good,' she offered. 'Because I don't think I could stand it if you were. He's such a bully, as are his sons. My family has known them for years. Did you know that he stormed into Sedeshire Hall, bawling at my father to call off this wedding?'

'I did not know that,' Lukas answered, and she got the impression he was fighting to keep his emotions in check.

She filed that away for later.

'What exactly did he tell your father?'

'I don't know.' She shrugged. 'I can't say that

I was listening. Though he was raging about my father betraying him.'

And then she waited for her new husband to fill in the gaps for which she was sure he had the pieces.

She told herself that she shouldn't be surprised when he merely shrugged, made his excuses and disappeared. Leaving her to greet the rest of their unimpressed guests alone.

'You can marry as many daughters of earls as you like—it won't make you any less of an illegitimate bastard.'

Lukas eyed the enraged, spluttering Andrew Rockman, Sixth Earl of Highmount, and forced down the bile that always threatened to drown him from the inside whenever he thought of him. The man who was—as much as Lukas would have cut out his own tongue before admitting it aloud—his biological father.

It took everything Lukas had to keep his voice even and light, as though those insulting words didn't resonate so deafeningly in his head. As though they didn't scrape inside him where he'd always felt so raw.

'I'm fairly certain that marrying as many daughters of earls as I like would make me a bigamist. But never fear, I only needed to marry the one in order for her father to give me a controlling share of Sedeshire International. The company you've been trying to get your grubby little paws on for years.'

He even offered a sardonic smile and was rewarded when the older man's eyes bulged with fury.

'You're an utter disgrace,' the Earl spat out.

'On the contrary, I'm a success. In business and now, it seems, in marriage. I may be an *illegitimate bastard*—' the words nearly lodged in Lukas's throat, but he made himself say them anyway '—yet to the world I'm the man who bagged an earl's daughter. And secured a company, all at once. Though I wonder what that says about my new father-in-law's loyalty to you? It's no secret that you've been desperate to get your greedy fingers on Sedeshire International, and yet he chose not to sell to you.'

'You're nothing!' the old Earl exploded viciously. 'A nobody.'

'Indeed, as your closest...' Lukas paused thoughtfully. 'Well, I wouldn't go so far as to call him a friend—I'm not certain that you understand the meaning of the term—so let's go with...ally. As your closest ally, I wonder what conclusions will be drawn from the fact that he agreed to marry Lady Octavia off to me, rather than one of your sons. Or, should I clarify, one of your legitimate sons.'

'You're no son of mine.'

For most of his life Lukas had chosen to tell

himself the same thing. It had suited him to pretend that he could not be connected to such a man—more than *suited him.* Denying the Earl's existence—even if only in his own head—had been as necessary to Lukas's well-being as learning to breathe. Now, though, seeing the old man's rage, Lukas felt compelled to fuel the fire.

'I couldn't agree more. Yet you can call me a *bastard,* just as you called my mother a whore, but it doesn't change the fact that we share the same blood.' The words almost curdled in his mouth, and Lukas made no attempt to disguise his contempt.

'Watch your tongue, boy,' the Earl snarled.

Lukas stood his ground. The old man might intimidate most people—even himself as a twelve-year-old boy carrying a message from his dying mother, only to be thrown, quite literally, from the Earl's home—but Lukas had long since learned how to stand up to bullies.

'One of your offspring is in prison for tax evasion, one can barely run his trust fund let alone a company, and the third has a reputation for plying young socialites with alcohol and drugs and then taking advantage.'

'Anyone who believes that will be made to pay,' the Earl hissed, as Lukas gave a bark of hollow laughter.

'Because you're a master at manipulating the truth, and getting people to lie for you? Just as my new wife's father lied for you when it came to the truth about my mother, and my parentage, all those years ago?' Lukas bunched his fists into his pockets as though that might control the grief and resentment that was rising inside his chest.

The older man sneered. 'Your new wife is as feeble and inadequate as your mother was. Another waste of a life.'

Lukas clenched his jaw so tight that he thought it might break. He had spent so many years resenting the fact that he'd had to look after his mother when, by rights, she should have been the one looking after him. Resenting her. Hating her, even. But he'd be damned if this oxygen thief standing in front of him needed to know that.

'You drove her to her grave,' Lukas managed. 'She told me how you tried to get her to terminate the pregnancy when you found out, then ensured she was left homeless and jobless when she refused.'

He might have known the Earl could sniff out any hint of weakness. The old man's eyes narrowed thoughtfully, then glinted.

'You think you know it all, don't you?' His smile was nothing short of brutal. 'But you don't know a thing, boy. You think she had morals, defying me to have you? You weren't her first baby. You're just the one that survived a failed attempt to get rid of you.'

'That's a lie.' The denial was out before Lukas

could stop it. Before his brain could kick in and warn him that this was exactly the reaction the man standing in front of him had wanted. Even now, the old man's eyes gleamed with victory.

'Oh, no lie.' He grinned, a cold, cruel baring of teeth. 'Your mother didn't want you any more than I did. She tried to rid herself of you, like I told her to. She always did what I told her to do. She never loved you, because there wasn't room in that weak, pathetic heart of hers for anyone but me. But, then, you already knew that, didn't you, boy?'

Lukas had no idea how he managed to hold himself together, let alone stopped himself from dropping the sorry excuse for a man to the ground. But he'd long ago learned to control that frustrated, angry streak that seemed to run through him and he wasn't about to give in to it now.

'I know that whatever she did was because you pushed her. You took advantage of a woman who loved you, so who was weaker and more pathetic? All you ever did was use her.'

The old man snorted in disdain. '*Love?* You talk of love, yet here I am, attending the wedding of my oldest friend's daughter and some upstart.' The Earl waved a gnarled hand at him. 'Not because you love her—you don't even know her— but because you wanted to steal their company from my grasp.'

'Octavia knew the deal from the start,' Lukas scorned. He had no intention of letting the old man know that the marriage part of the deal wasn't exactly concerned with the business side. 'I didn't make her believe I cared, only to then use her. Unlike the way you treated my mother, my new bride knew the circumstances of the agreement all along.'

But still it didn't stop those cold fingers of apprehension from slinking down his spine. The image of her walking down the aisle in her father's grip.

'You tell yourself that so that you can believe you're better than me. But you'll ruin her all the same. You don't have it in you not to do so. You're no better than a mangy dog from the gutter.'

'You're mellowing in your old age,' Lukas mocked. 'You managed far crueller put-downs when I was a kid. You, the bully who took such delight in mocking a twelve-year-old boy— telling me that I should stay in the gutter, where I belonged, that I would never amount to anything. I've no doubt you comfort yourself daily with the notion that landed gentry isn't true nobility.'

'And if I hadn't mocked you, would you have been so driven to get to where you are today? That dirty, worthless kid would never have had it in him to make it this far. Perhaps you should be thanking me for giving you the drive that you so sorely needed back then.'

The Earl stopped thoughtfully as some of the contempt faded from his expression. 'You're focused and ruthless, just like me. Perhaps the apple didn't fall too far from the tree after all.'

Loathing coursed through Lukas. 'I'm nothing like you,' he ground out, appalled.

He hated that that only seemed to make the Earl all the more exultant.

'You're more like me than you might think. And, as much as you might hate me, I have no doubt that one day it will be you standing where I am, and some bastard kid of yours standing where you are, staring at you with the same deep loathing.'

'I will never have kids,' Lukas refuted. 'No child deserves to have your tainted blood running through its veins.'

'You have fire, boy. Perhaps I shouldn't have been so quick to throw you out of my house all those years ago. Maybe you're worthy of the Rockman name and title after all.'

'I don't need your title.' Lukas gritted his teeth. 'I have my own. What's more, I worked for mine. You don't get to claim credit for it.'

The Earl curled his lip. 'You have a knighthood. As quaint as that is, it's no peerage. And I blocked you in that when I refused to acknowledge your mother.'

'Which is the only thing you recognise, isn't it?' Lukas disparaged. 'Have you ever considered that one day I might find a way to prove you lied all those years ago?'

Lukas couldn't be sure if it was the mere threat or if the Earl had begun to piece it together, but, either way, the old man looked as though he was about to lose his mind, right there in that anteroom…right up until he dropped to the ground like a sack of potatoes.

It was odd how there was no warning. No clutching of his chest. No calling out. One moment the Earl was standing in front of Lukas, and the next moment the man simply toppled to the ground as if his legs had suddenly gone from under him. For a moment Lukas could only look on, stunned. A part of him even suspected it was some new ploy by the old man. But there was just silence.

Not quite believing what was happening, Lukas dropped to his heels and reached out to check the Earl's pulse.

There wasn't one.

For a fraction of a second Lukas thought he might actually have considered just walking away. Just leaving this man who had caused him—and his mother, as weak as she had been— so much unnecessary pain. How many times over the years had he wished this man dead?

But then instinct cut in and, with a low curse, Lukas hurried to the door, flung it open and bellowed down the empty corridor for one of the hotel staff. Then, moving quickly back across the room, he dropped onto his knees and began chest compressions.

Oti was in the Grosvenor Wing, gritting her teeth as she greeted the guests alone, wondering if she'd already been ditched—with a cluster of sombre-looking female Z-list guests who would have loved that to have been the case—when she heard Lukas's shout, as faint as it was in the main hall.

She wondered what it said about how tuned-in she was to her fake husband, as she slid through the oblivious crowd and hurried along an endless plushly carpeted corridor. She only knew she was heading in the right direction because a couple of members of staff were ducking into a room a little ahead of her.

Silently lamenting the weight and encumbrance of her dress's long train, Oti surged after them.

'Lukas? Did you...? Oh, good grief.'

He glanced up and she wished she could read the expression that flickered in his eyes when he saw her. But then it was gone, and Lukas was all business.

'Call for an ambulance. He collapsed less than a minute ago—there was no indication.' Lukas didn't miss a compression. 'He isn't breathing, and he has no pulse.'

Oti didn't wait to hear any more. Pushing through the dithering hotel staff, she circled the patient—only then realising the man's identity—and knelt down on the other side to Lukas and carried out her own brief assessment.

'I'll do the rescue breathing if you want to continue with compressions.' She glanced up at the still staring staff, starting with a young man. 'Right, you go and call an ambulance *now* and tell them that we've begun CPR. *Go!* And you—does the hotel have a defibrillator?'

As the young man stumbled away, the girl blinked at her.

'I need you to stop panicking and think.' Oti kept her tone calm but firm. 'If you don't know, then I need you to go straight to your manager and ask. A defibrillator, understand? Also, ask if you keep shots of epinephrine. Got it? Now you need to hurry.'

She jerked her head shakily then turned and hurried out of the room. Oti could only hope that the girl could hold herself together long enough to get what they needed.

Briefly, she wondered what had been so urgent that Lukas and Andrew Rockman had been discussing it alone. Certainly without her father. But she could contemplate that later. Right now, she had to focus on working with Lukas to save the man's life. Even if a part of her suspected the world would be a better place without the likes of the Earl of Highmount. The current one, or the son who would inherit the title if Andrew were to die.

For the next five minutes she and Lukas worked together, soon establishing a surprisingly efficient rhythm until the girl returned with the defibrillator, and what looked like a manager.

'The ambulance is on its way, and I've sent someone to stand at the entrance to bring them straight here.'

'Great.' Oti nodded, her eyes not leaving the patient as she silently counted Lukas's compressions. 'Okay, turn the defib on.'

'I don't know how to use it.' The manager shook his head. 'We only got it last week and training isn't until next week.'

Bending her head, Oti was unable to answer as she began two short rescue breaths.

'It's okay—I know,' Lukas muttered. 'Just turn the machine on and follow the instructions on the read-out whilst I complete one more cycle of compressions, then you can hand the defib to me.'

Finishing the rescue breaths, Oti sat up as Lukas began compressions again. When the Earl's life was on the line, was it right for her to allow Lukas to take charge, just to preserve her own secret?

Watching Lukas working on the older man, Oti weighed up her options. Clearly, he knew what he was doing in terms of the pace and pressure of the chest compressions—and although it was a draining task he made it look deceptively easy—which was good to see, but using the defib could be a different story.

'…twenty-eight, twenty-nine, thirty.'

As Oti bent her head for another two rescue breaths, she was aware of the manager handing the defib to Lukas, who, having already unbuttoned the Earl's shirt, removed the sticky pads and began to place them down on the man's bare chest. A perfect position for the one beneath the right clavicle, but the other one was slightly off. There was nothing else for it.

'Wait.' She reached out to stay his hand, fighting off the jolt of awareness that shot through her at the contact.

And it had nothing to do with the defibrillator.

Valiantly trying to ignore it, Oti guided his hand a few centimetres lower and set it down.

'What do you think you're doing?' She was sure that it wasn't just her imagination that his voice sounded hoarser.

'Moving you to a more lateral position.' She shook her head, struggling to regroup. 'Even amongst medical professionals, the location of the apical pad can often be too medial.' She barely recognised her own voice. 'The result is reduced separation between the pads, causing the current to pass through non-cardiac tissue and potentially reducing the successfulness of the defibrillation.'

He eyed her intently for a brief moment and she thought he was going to say something more. Instead, he merely inclined his head.

'You sound like you know better than I do.'

She told herself that it was good that he wasn't so full of his own self-importance that he refused to listen to her, but she shouldn't feel so ridiculously flattered.

Attaching the pad to the Earl's chest, she turned her attention back to the machine as it analysed their patient's heartbeat.

'Stand clear.' She glanced at Lukas, but he'd already edged back a little from the man, his hands up to indicate he was no longer in contact. 'Shocking.'

As the machine delivered a shock, Oti waited long enough to check the read-out before setting it aside and continuing CPR.

Lukas matched her without a word, as if they were in perfect sync. As if he was someone she'd worked with for years. But she didn't allow herself to consider it any further.

For a couple more minutes they continued CPR, with Oti giving two breaths for every thirty compressions from Lukas. After five cycles she delivered a second shock to the Earl, and more compressions, but still to no effect.

'Any idea on the ambulance?' she demanded, turning to the manager, who was on his walkie-talkie and looking rather ashen himself.

'It's coming down the lanes now…a minute or so out.'

'Yes.' She nodded, though her eyes didn't leave the patient as Lukas began.

So a good few minutes before they got to the patient. Another cycle and another shock by her and Lukas, and if that wasn't successful, at least they should be able to administer epinephrine before administering a fourth shock.

And one thought niggled at her. If the Earl should need an IV, given the shape that he was in, her recommendation would have to be an intraosseous infusion for a non-collapsible entry point, since intravenous wouldn't be feasible. And what if the crew weren't trained for IO? She could end up having to administer it herself. How many questions would that raise with her new husband?

'Another set?' Lukas said grimly, interrupting her thoughts, half a command, half a question.

Blinking, she took a moment to reassess.

'Yes.' Oti nodded at last. 'Another set.'

For the next few minutes they resumed their roles, the time passing all too fast before she administered another shock. Then, abruptly, the old Earl's heart kicked back in, just as the ambulance crew hurried into the room.

For the next few moments Oti was occupied with handing over in a timely manner, relieved that they accepted what she and Lukas had done as though there were quasi-trained guests, rather than her being a doctor.

And still Oti couldn't work out whether Lukas was happy that they'd been successful in saving the Earl's life—or not.

'What were you talking about in that room, anyway?' she attempted casually. She might have known Lukas wouldn't fall for it.

'Who says we were talking?'

'He didn't want me to marry you,' she commented instead, and she thought it said a lot that he didn't pretend not to know who she was talking about.

She tried to recall the argument between Andrew Rockman and her father that evening, wishing that she hadn't dismissed it at the time, but little that her father did interested her. She had even less interest in what the Rockman family did.

Now her brain was beginning to whirl, throwing up snippets of old information that she'd thought the two older men would long since have forgotten about.

'They were arguing about the past.' She bit her lip thoughtfully. 'A group of hotel chains and luxury boutiques that the Rockman family once owned, until they lost it all in a hostile takeover.'

It had been a successful chain but, instead of trading on the name, by all accounts it had been stripped down methodically and ruthlessly. Andrew Rockman had always claimed that it had been about more than business, that it had been personal. Some young upstart targeting him.

Now she couldn't stop herself from asking Lukas if he had been that upstart.

'What else do you remember?' Lukas demanded, which wasn't the answer Oti had been expecting, yet it was somehow more of an answer.

'Not a lot more.' She shrugged. 'I'm afraid I wasn't exactly paying attention. Ten years ago I *was* that party girl you accused me of still being.'

She eyed him defiantly, but he didn't offer a put-down this time. Not that it made her feel any less ashamed when she thought back to the way she'd spent her life schlepping from one luxury beach holiday to the next. From a party on some billionaire's yacht to a celebration in Monaco. Between the ages of fifteen and nineteen, she'd played the part of the airheaded socialite only too shamefully well. She could hardly blame Lukas for thinking she was still that girl. It had been nearly a decade and yet the rest of her so-called social circle had never let her forget it.

'And ten years ago I was that young upstart,' Lukas ground out unexpectedly. 'We both have a past, Octavia. The point now is to make this marriage—this business transaction—work for us. Are you prepared to do that?'

She was still reeling from her new husband's shock revelation, her brain still trying to piece it together. It was as though she was seeing tiny sections but missing the big picture.

'I am prepared,' she offered at length. 'So what now?'

'Now we get through the next few hours and then I'll drop you off back home. My home,' he clarified tightly.

'Drop me off?' Oti frowned. 'Where are you going?'

Her skin was starting to prickle at his unexpected change of tone as she frantically tried to work out what had just happened. He was no longer the teasing, amused Lukas of before. Now he was sharper, colder, more withdrawn. And it shouldn't have mattered to her.

But it did.

'I have conference calls to attend to,' he told her coolly. 'Work doesn't stop just because today is my wedding day.'

'Heaven forbid,' she remarked, but he didn't even crack a smile. 'And what about me? What should I do?'

Lukas looked almost disdainful. 'You should do…whatever it is that you do.'

And even as she told herself that she should be glad she'd just been presented with the perfect opportunity to visit Edward—the brother who she hated having to pretend had died in that accident—she was powerless to stop a sting of hurt from working its way under her skin.

CHAPTER FOUR

'Look, I've done my research.' Oti eyed her brother. 'I've used every contact I could as a doctor, to really make sure, and I truly believe you're a perfect candidate. Nerve transfer surgery has a high success rate for C5 to C6 spinal cord injuries.'

'But it won't make me walk again,' Edward threw back.

It sliced right through her to hear him so uncharacteristically angry and bitter. Not that she blamed him—how could she?—but the Edward she'd known and loved had always been ready with a light-hearted quip or a joke to lighten the moment.

She missed that Edward, more than she liked to admit.

She *needed* her brother back. For all that their father had ever put them through, they'd always had each other. For support, for counsel, or even for simple sibling teasing. But the accident hadn't just robbed Edward of his ability to walk or move; it had also robbed him of his sense of self.

And it had robbed her of her big brother.

Without him, she'd felt more alone these past four years than she could have imagined.

Before she could catch herself, Oti reached for her wedding rings, as though to twirl them on her finger the way she had done virtually all last night, unable to sleep. But she'd removed her rings before visiting Edward—he would have spotted them instantly and demanded to know about them, and she'd never been able to lie to her big brother.

But it was disconcerting how bare her hand felt without them. After less than twenty-four hours. Oti didn't care to examine what that said about her. She forced her focus back to Edward.

'No, it won't help you to walk again,' she agreed evenly. 'But this procedure could allow you to regain use of your arms. You might be able to lift a cup and feed yourself. You could be able to lift your arms above your head to dress yourself, or even turn on a light switch. Maybe you could even have enough strength to turn a door handle and push your own wheelchair. You could even make one of your godawful peanut butter sandwiches, which always glued my tongue to the roof of my mouth. You could be independent again, Edward. You wouldn't have to have carers on hand 24/7. Feeding you, cleaning you, even having to scratch your damned nose for you if it itches. I know how you hate it. But, this way, you could get some quality of life back.'

'Could. Might. Maybe...' He echoed the words hollowly. 'Do you hear yourself?'

It broke her heart, but she couldn't afford to let him see that. This was Edward, her incredible brother, who had been able to do anything. *Every*thing. He was tough and he wasn't a quitter. He never had been.

She just had to bring that back out of him now.

'Oh, I'm sorry, did you have some better plan?' she forced herself to say. 'My mistake. I see your life is just how you want it right now.'

'Funny,' he threw at her.

But she was sure she saw just a glint of something in his eyes. As though the old Edward was still in there—somewhere. It was more than she'd seen in four years. But, then, this was the first time she'd been able to give him something akin to hope in the past four years.

She made herself press on. 'Or you could just give up, of course. Prove Father right and be the quitter he keeps saying you are. Is that what you want, Edward? To let him win by giving up on yourself? On me? On your own life?'

For one long, horrible moment he stared at her and Oti felt the words of apology racing up through her, ready to spill out everywhere. And then, all of a sudden, he offered a twisted kind of smile.

It wasn't perfect, but it was better than nothing.

'Who the hell wants to let that repulsive old bully win anything?'

'Right.' She hesitated. It wasn't exactly the re-sounding agreement she'd hoped for. But neither was it the stonewalling for which she'd been pre-paring herself.

She waited as the silence enveloped them again. Should she say something more? Or wait for Edward to speak?

Oti clenched her fingers together in her lap and forced herself to be patient. If Edward was going to go for it, he would need to be the one to instigate it.

'Nerve transfers aren't new,' he pointed out, after what seemed like a lifetime. 'But they've never really been successful on spinal cord in-juries.'

'You know about them?'

He snorted loudly. 'You think I haven't con-stantly looked for new procedures, sitting here in this damned chair all day, unable to even lift my own glass of water to drink?'

It was all Oti could do not to smile. Or cry. Possibly both. Instead, she focused on keeping her emotions in check and her voice even. Ed-ward wouldn't thank her for a song and dance— though he might enjoy the irony of her pun—and, in any case, she didn't want to oversell it.

There were still no guarantees, after all.

She moved around the table, sitting down carefully and trying not to look too eager. And all the while pushing to the back of her mind that all this hinged on their father honouring his agreement to her and paying for the surgery.

Looking at her brother's face, agreeing to marry Lukas in return seemed like a small price to pay.

She wasn't an idiot. Her father would have always found someone to marry her off to—and some way to have leverage over her to do so. She was lucky it was Lukas and not one of his boorish friends. Or one of their hard-partying sons.

And it wasn't as though she had someone of her own to love. Not that she wouldn't have liked that…but her social circle, and her job, made that rather difficult.

She ignored the sensation that rippled through her when she thought of Lukas. A fleeting chemical attraction. Nothing more.

'It's a combination of nerve transfer for dexterity, and tendon transfer for strength. Both of these are well-established procedures, just for other areas. For example, tendon transfer is well described in the area of hand surgeries.'

'I need upper arm strength.'

'Right,' Oti agreed. 'So they would remove a working nerve from a donor site in the shoulder, close to the damaged section of nerve preventing the signal from reaching the lower arm, and then use that working nerve to effectively bypass the damaged section. Then it is connected back to the spinal cord. But where, previously, they might have used one donor, here we would be talking about two, or even multiple.'

'And then I can move my arms again. As if by magic,' Edward ground out, getting angry again, his bitterness intertwined with frustration and sheer exhaustion.

She couldn't blame him; she could only imagine what he was going through. He'd been like this for the better part of four years.

Oti weighed her options. She could go in gently, or she could see if the tough love option was still her best bet.

'Not by magic,' she told him firmly. 'The surgery is just the start of it. After that you have months of rehab and hard work.'

'Sounds appealing,' her brother gritted out.

'Or years of rehab, if you don't put in the effort.'

He didn't answer for a moment. But when he finally did speak, Oti wasn't prepared for it.

'So, what you're saying is that I'm going to need to put my back into it.'

She blinked at him.

'But I will,' he continued, deadpan. 'Because I know that you, my sweet baby sister, will have my back.'

'Hilarious,' she managed, still shocked.

It was a terrible pun, but she wasn't sure she cared. It had been so long since Edward had made a joke about anything—certainly not his disability—that she couldn't help feeling this was progress.

It was certainly better than calling himself a *head on a stick.*

She thought that particular self-description had broken her heart worst of all.

'Edward…'

'It's going to be just *spine.*'

And then, without warning, he laughed.

It was a slightly stiff, awkward laugh. But it was a laugh all the same. And Oti didn't know if it was hearing Edward make bad puns, or the emotion of her marriage to Lukas—or perhaps it was the fact that she knew she never could have dreamt of offering Edward this glimmer of hope had she failed to go through with the marriage to Lukas—but she lost it.

It rushed over her and she dropped her head in her hands and sobbed.

'Don't cry, Oats,' Edward growled.

He hadn't called her by that childhood nickname for years. Somehow, that only made her cry a little harder.

'Please, Oats,' her brother tried again after a moment. 'I feel useless—I can't give you a hug. I can't even take your hand.'

Sniffing hard, half crying and half laughing,

she took his hand. What she wouldn't give to have her brother haul her into one of his old bear-like hugs and tell her everything would be okay.

But he couldn't.

And she needed to be the one to be strong for him. There was no one to be strong for her.

Lukas?

The question popped, unbidden, into her brain. Oti stuffed it back down hastily.

Lukas Woods couldn't be trusted with the truth.

No one could.

'Sorry.' Pulling herself together, Oti wiped her arm across her eyes. 'It's just been a long couple of days. But it's done now. So let's get back to the rehab after your operation.'

'The gruelling bit, you said.'

'True. But since when were you ever bothered by a little hard work, Edward?'

'I'm not.' He blew out a frustrated breath. 'But do you really think they'll take me on, Oats? The candidates they've chosen were all less than eighteen months post-spinal-cord accident. I'm nearly five years.'

'They're making strides with it all the time, Edward.' She focused on her brother. 'The experiences they had with the first few groups have informed their understanding of the procedures. Of nerve topography itself.'

'Which means…?'

'It means they studied how spasticity allows preserved muscle function and stops atrophy.'

'I have no idea what you're saying to me.' Edward frowned. 'You might as well be speaking Sudanese for all I know.'

'Nuer,' she corrected absently. 'Or Dinka.'

'Which raises another question,' Edward cut in. 'These trials are new, and I don't qualify for any current clinical trials, which means we'd have to pay for this surgery.'

Oti schooled herself not to panic. 'No, there's a new trial...'

'There isn't.' He stopped her again. 'How are you intending to pay for this, Oats? Because volunteering as a doctor in Sub-Saharan Africa might feed your soul, little sister, but it doesn't do much for your wallet. And I don't have anything since Father seized control of my company after the accident. If I hadn't had private insurance, I wouldn't even have this place.'

'Father will...'

'Spare me,' Edward snorted. 'He wouldn't throw a pound my way even if he had it. Which he doesn't, given that he's gambled away everything owned by the Sedeshire estate, bar the damned Hall itself.'

'He's...made some money.' Oti tried to sound convincing, but she'd never found it easy to lie to her big brother.

It was one of the reasons she worked in

Africa—to avoid having to lie to his face. That, and the fact that he'd banned her from visiting for the first couple of years after the accident, and she hadn't been able to stand being just down the road from his hospital whilst he'd refused to even see her.

The fact that their father had been only too inexplicably happy to wash his hands of a tetraplegic son had only heightened her sense of injustice.

As though, somehow, the Earl felt that Edward's lack of mobility might somehow reflect on his own image of apparent virility.

How many more ways could their father have left to disappoint either of his children?

'No, he hasn't,' Edward contradicted smoothly. 'If he had, he'd have gambled it away again faster than you could say *Quit whilst you're ahead.*'

He pinned her with a sharp stare, and it was all Oti could do not to squirm. She smoothed down her grey jersey trousers, picking off a sliver of some imaginary lint.

'What gives, Oats?'

A hundred different excuses darted around her head, though nothing that she thought her brother might believe. But then he spoke again, his voice cracking as he asked her not to bring him hope of an operation there was no chance they could afford.

'Of course not. I wouldn't...' The words tumbled out in her horror. 'Trust me. We can afford the operation.'

'How?'

Another skewering gaze. Her heart pounded in her chest. There was nothing else for it but to come clean.

'I got married.'

He didn't answer; he simply stared at her. And that was worse, somehow. Without knowing what she was doing, Oti reached inside her pocket and retrieved her wedding rings and slid them nervously back onto her finger.

It shouldn't have felt so...*comforting* to do so.

'You got married?' Edward managed at last, his expression little short of thunderous. 'For me?'

'No,' she lied, far more smoothly than she might have thought possible.

'For me,' he confirmed in sheer disgust. 'Not one of those lecherous old sops Father kept pushing you to marry, just so his own debts could be expunged?'

'No.'

'Not Louis Rockman?' Edward's face twisted. 'After what he tried to do to you as a kid?'

'No.' Oti couldn't suppress a shudder at the thought. 'He's a successful businessman. And he's...*nice.*'

And there was no reason at all for her to feel quite so guarded.

'But he's still paying Father off, isn't he?' Edward demanded harshly.

'Yes, but this time I made him promise to pay for this surgery.'

Her brother snorted. 'He'll never honour it. You know that.'

'He'll have to—it's written into the contract,' she lied.

'So you see,' she continued loftily, 'everyone wins. I can't be married off twice.'

Her father might try it, of course, but once Edward had undergone the surgery, the old Earl would have no more leverage over her.

'And at least this way it's someone with whom I can actually stand to be in the same room,' she continued when Edward still didn't reply.

It was supposed to be an explanation that would placate her brother but, even as she said the words, Oti realised there was a grain of truth in it.

A memory of Lukas in the cathedral, and that kiss, lit up her brain as heat flushed through her.

Okay, more than a grain, then.

'Who is it?' Edward demanded abruptly, his eyes raking over her face. 'Which of his cronies did he force you to marry, Oats?'

She fought to compose herself.

'Lukas Woods.'

He stared at her for such a long moment that

she wasn't sure if he'd actually heard her. And then he spluttered with disbelief, *'Lukas Woods?'*

'He's...'

'You can't be serious, Oats?'

Well, at least he wasn't back to calling her Octavia, which meant he couldn't be *that* mad. Now that she considered it, he didn't look even half as cross as she might have expected.

'Have you ever met him?' She wasn't sure what made her ask the question, but she hadn't really expected it to be true.

'I have, actually. Yes. A couple of times, several years ago. Once at a business event, and once at the racetrack.'

'Lukas races cars, like you?' she asked, before catching herself. 'Like you used to do.'

'No, he was more into the mechanics side. He liked to build them, and just raced to see how they performed. He told me one of his first jobs was for a car mechanic when he was a kid, and in his spare time he used to go to the scrapyard and he used what he could find to build old engines. I guess when his company took off he kept it going as a hobby.'

But a serious hobby, by the sound of it. Just like Edward's racing used to be.

Her first thought was that she liked the fact that her brother kind of liked Lukas. Her second was that it shouldn't matter what her big brother thought.

'I thought he was a decent bloke. So why did Woods marry you? What did he get out of the deal?'

She didn't want to tell him, but at the same time she couldn't bring herself to lie to him.

'Father sold him a controlling interest in Sedeshire International.'

For a moment Edward dropped his head down and her heart suddenly lurched. His hair would once have fallen in his eyes when he did that, and he'd had this habit of thrusting his fingers into it to rake it back. It was a mannerism that she'd never really paid attention to before. But now he couldn't even lift his arm to do that. And his hair was so short that it didn't move a single millimetre when his head moved.

God, how she missed such a simple gesture.

'Well, if my company had to go, better it's in Woods's hands than in Father's.'

'Or Andrew Rockman's,' she told him quietly.

'Christ, is that who else was interested?'

She nodded slowly.

'Then yeah.' He sounded resigned. 'Definitely better with Lukas Woods. But you shouldn't have married him. He might be a decent bloke to another bloke, but he isn't who I would want my baby sister marrying. Why did you do it, Oats?'

'Because it was either him or Louis Rockman. Can we discuss that later?' She tried to smooth things over. 'I just want to focus on you right now.'

'Forget it, Oti.' Edward blew out a breath and her heart ached that he was thinking of her even as he must be seeing his own chance—however slim—at some degree of recovery slipping away.

She reached forward, catching herself as she was about to put her hand over his—he wouldn't even feel her—and moving it to his cheek instead.

'Too late, Edward.' Her voice was soft. 'I already married him. The deed is done. So unless you want a bully like Father to be the only one to win, then you might as well accept it.'

'No, Oti.'

'You have to.' Frustration, and an old sense of guilt, bubbled up inside her, leaving her helpless to control her outburst. 'You wouldn't be in this state if it hadn't been for me.'

He blew out a sharp breath. 'For pity's sake, you weren't driving. I was. You weren't even in the car with me.'

'But if you hadn't been racing to collect me...' She splayed her hands. 'If I hadn't called you, panicking, because *he* was at that party...'

'Stop it, Oats. It wasn't your fault.'

'It *was* my fault.' Oti let her head drop, her throat tight and clogged. 'If I'd never called you...'

'So what happens if I have a lower motor neuron intact?' he asked abruptly.

'What?' She jerked her head up, confused.

'Tell me about the procedure,' Edward ground out.

He was making an effort again. Pulling himself together despite everything. And she needed to do the same.

Oti smiled a watery smile. This was precisely why it didn't matter what she'd had to promise to Lukas, or her father.

Edward was worth it.

'Then the peripheral nerve transfer procedure can work to reroute expendable donors to non-functional nerves.'

For the next hour or so they talked through options and procedures. And it felt promising that Edward was listening to her, and they weren't fighting any more.

All that was left to do now was to call her father and get the funds he'd agreed to give her. She would do it as soon as she left Edward.

Her father must have received the money by now. The deal had stipulated that it be transferred to him from Lukas the moment they walked out of that cathedral as husband and wife. And—the Roc Holdings takeover aside—Lukas had a reputation for being utterly scrupulous where business was concerned.

She hoped with every fibre of her being that

her father would honour the deal. Because if Lukas was softening towards her at all—and maybe it was just fancifulness on her part to think that was the case—then he wasn't going to feel that way if she had to go to him to try to inveigle more money out of him.

It would make her seem, certainly in Lukas's eyes, as greedy and grasping as her father himself.

CHAPTER FIVE

'CARE TO TELL me where you've been?'

Oti jumped as she closed the door to her suite. Slowly, she turned to look at Lukas as he stood— he felt as though he'd been lurking—by the connecting doors.

The expression in her stunning blue eyes was like a hand reaching inside his chest and clutching that thing which passed for a heart. Then twisting.

'What is it, Octavia?'

He heard the words before it even registered that he'd been going to say them, and he didn't like it that her eyes widened, as if the concern in his tone surprised her. As though she didn't expect kindness from him.

He fought back a wave of what felt astonishingly like…remorse.

'I was just…' She shook her head, clearly rattled. 'I phoned my father.'

'Oh…?' he prompted when she fell abruptly silent.

She didn't answer. Lukas wasn't even certain that she'd heard him.

'Octavia?'

She jerked her head up, her gaze colliding with his again. And then…something changed. The air around her shifted. She shook her head back so that her glorious curtain of hair danced over her shoulders, and with almost controlled deliberation she sashayed into the bedroom and past where he stood, wholly unconcerned.

'To answer your original question, I've been out,' she replied casually.

A feral growl rumbled up through his body. 'I can see that,' he said. 'Out where?'

'Who are you? My father?'

She almost laughed as she dropped her bag on the chair, began to unwind the long scarf from around her neck and removed her earrings, whilst he watched transfixed and feeling downright murderous.

'No, Octavia.' He let the doors go with a sweep of his arms, then stalked into the room. 'I'm your husband. Or do you need a reminder about that?'

And then he felt shocked at how jealous he was. As though he didn't know whether he was more annoyed at her or disgusted with himself. Perhaps because he hadn't been able to chase images of her wearing nothing but some scraps of snow-white lace, that he'd ached to tear off with his teeth, for God's sake—out of his head.

He'd actually convinced himself that he'd succeeded. All day at work he'd pretended to himself that he'd pushed her from his head, only to return home this evening to find the place distinctly Octavia-free and his driver gone.

It had felt inexplicably empty.

And now she'd practically floated back in, with a glow that he recognised from the women he'd slept with in the past. Only...he hadn't slept with her, which meant only one thing.

And a kind of primal rage seethed through his veins, even as he told himself that he didn't care.

That he *shouldn't* care.

But ever since their damned kiss at the altar he'd felt as edgy as an adolescent. Unfocused in an important business meeting today, and unable to distract himself with even the more herculean of physical exercise.

'I know you're my husband,' she said calmly, snapping him back to reality. 'We were married less than twenty-four hours ago—I'm hardly likely to forget.'

'So where were you?' he growled, not even recognising himself.

What was it about her that had him turning himself inside out?

She lowered her hands to her lap so damned calmly that it scraped at him all the more. Then she cocked her head towards him.

'Why do you care?'

Lukas didn't answer. Words would have been impossible. He wasn't just angry; he was furious. Emotions that were unfamiliar, and certainly unappreciated, surged through him. He didn't even know what he was doing.

Fake marriage or not, out of respect he had decided not to indulge in extramarital affairs. He'd at least expected her to show the same courtesy.

They'd only just had the ceremony, and it was about the optics of the situation.

Yeah, right...the optics.

Thrusting aside the unwelcome voice, Lukas forced himself to move to a chair, throwing himself down with his usual insouciance and stretching his arms out behind his head. No need for his deceitful new bride to know just how pent-up he was.

But then he watched as her eyes followed the line of his chest, as though drawn there against her will. That tiny intake of breath. The flicker of her tongue over her lips. It appalled and thrilled him in equal measure.

That attraction between them was still there. That was something. He could use that to his advantage.

Is that all it is? a voice taunted inside his head.

Lukas chose to ignore it.

'Perhaps I failed to be clear before, but I am very protective of what is mine. And since, as you so conveniently pointed out a few moments ago, we only married yesterday.'

'Is that so?' She surprised him. 'I didn't think we would be playing by those rules.'

'Well, we are.'

'Both of us?' she demanded. 'Or just me?'

For a long moment Lukas stared at her. And slowly he began to realise what was going on, the truth of it making him want to jump up and punch the air in triumph.

Inexplicably.

'Is that what this is about?' He grinned. And she blinked at him as though she wasn't sure how or why the tables had turned. 'Tit for tat? You think I'll cat around, so you're getting your kicks in first?'

'I *think* you'll cat around?' she echoed scornfully, doing a half-decent job of pretending that she was aghast, in Lukas's opinion. 'I don't *think* it, Lukas. I *know* it. Look at your reputation.'

'And so you intend to do the same?' He wasn't sure how he managed to stay in his seat.

Especially when she shrugged so easily.

'Why not?'

'This will not continue now that we are married,' he told her. Serenely.

Taking it as a victory that she stiffened perceptibly.

'I beg your pardon?'

Another flash of a smile that felt too sharp on

his own mouth. He didn't understand what he was doing, or why he felt so...*outside* himself. But it didn't seem to matter. The words were coming out, anyway.

'Whoever you met this afternoon, you will not meet him again. Do you understand?'

'I know your reputation,' she continued too evenly, as she casually plucked a tiny piece of non-existent lint from those deliciously backside-hugging jersey trousers.

It was a habit of hers he'd noticed right from that first night, five months ago. Though he couldn't have said why he'd been so paying so much attention.

'The whole world knows it, of course.' She was still speaking, frowning at him. 'And it isn't what a new bride would like to hear.'

'Is that so?' Lukas demanded, that full mouth of hers...*doing things* to him.

He told himself it was the whisky still running through his veins from the limo drive home, though he suspected that was not actually the source of his perturbation. He'd probably sweated that out after the first couple of hours of beasting himself.

Across from him, Oti lifted her shoulders as elegantly as she possibly could.

'You like to live life to its fullest. You drink and gamble and carouse.'

'Carouse?'

Her eyes narrowed at him. 'Now you wish to take issue with my choice of words?'

Despite everything, amusement tugged at the corners of his mouth. 'Forgive me, *Lady* Octavia.'

She glowered at him, and he liked that rather more than he ought to.

'My point is,' she emphasised irritably, 'that you are infamous for having a string of lovers. So I would ask whether you intend for your endless string of affairs and flings to continue?'

It was puzzling how little the idea appealed to him suddenly.

'Does it matter?'

'It does when you're dictating who I may and may not meet now that we are married. Sauce for the goose and all that.'

'There will be no sauce,' he ground out, barely able to focus. His head was being turned inside out. 'No taking my driver to meet other men. No affairs.'

'And you?' she pressed. 'Not that I care about the affairs per se, of course. More that I don't wish to be made to look a fool any more than it appears you do.'

She leaned back on the bed then, her arms extended behind her. Lukas suspected she had no idea how that put her breasts on display in that figure-hugging top. Less idea still of quite how her gentle unpretentiousness was affecting him.

He'd never much cared for *sweet* women before, preferring those who knew what they were getting themselves into with him. He desired women, sure, and he prided himself on being a thorough, generous lover. But he'd never been so preoccupied with fantasies about peeling their clothes off, slowly and delicately. Taking such time and care.

It was all that had consumed his thoughts ever since she'd hauled that insane wedding dress around his house last night.

Ever since he'd opened that door and seen her standing there in those scraps of lace like some kind of real-life erotic pin-up.

'Are you offering yourself as an alternative?' His voice was little more than a rasp as he deliberately avoided her question.

He barely recognised himself. Or the primal creature that howled inside him, making him take one step, and then another, getting all too close to where she sat. To the *bed* on which she sat.

And he found that he felt altogether too much like an untried, overeager adolescent.

'If you want me to yourself, *my lady*, then you need only say so.'

She laughed, a sensual sound that seemed to wind itself around his groin like a fist. A very soft but firm Octavia-style fist.

What the hell was wrong with him? He didn't even *want* to want her. She was everything he despised. From her lifestyle to her morals. And whilst that might be okay for a single night of mutual satisfaction with a woman he would never have to see again, it wasn't a good idea to complicate things in this clear-cut arrangement of theirs. Why blur the lines with a woman he would have to see day in, day out for the foreseeable future?

And still he kept advancing.

'I realise you may find this difficult to understand, given the sheer volume of women who follow you around just hoping you'll notice them for a night, but you are not at all my type, Lukas. I am not the slightest bit attracted to you.'

Victory smashed through him. It made him want to punch his hand into the air.

Because here, at last, he finally knew she was lying.

He knew women, and he knew how his new bride had looked at him. Yesterday, on their wedding day and the first time they had met. She might not like him much, and she might like his reputation even less, but she *was* attracted to him. She couldn't help herself any more than he could. It was apparent in every line of that lush body of hers.

'I know you want me,' he rumbled, revelling in this sensation that was moving through him. 'I can read it in the way you respond to me. Every time. You can't help yourself.'

'I don't do any such thing,' she argued, but her voice was faltering. Insubstantial.

A revelation.

'Would you care to put that to the test?' he asked gruffly, the ache stirring inside him all the more.

There was a beat of hesitation before she answered. 'What kind of test?'

A thousand thoughts raced through his head. Each one dirtier than the last. He reined them in quickly.

'A kiss,' he told her simply.

'A kiss?' Her eyes raked over him searchingly. It might as well have been her fingertips.

He shivered.

'Yes,' he confirmed. 'If you respond, you'll admit the attraction. If you don't respond… Well, that won't happen.'

'Such humility,' she needled. But her eyebrows knitted together, as if she was trying to see the catch. 'That's it?'

'That's it,' he confirmed, willing her to accept.

When was the last time he'd wanted anything so much?

Oti pursed her lips, her brow pulling tighter as she tried to decide whether she could deceive him.

He didn't know why he held his breath, willing her to bite. And then she lifted her head and jerked her chin to him defiantly.

'Sure, why not? One kiss to prove you wrong.'

It was almost comical, the way she sat up,

folded her hands into their usual place on her lap and closed her eyes as she tilted her head to the side.

Before he could think better of it, Lukas scooped her up and lifted her off the bed.

'Wait—where are we going?'

Wordlessly, he carried her out of her bedroom and to the sitting area, before sinking onto one of the couches with Octavia sprawled in his lap.

She struggled to right herself. 'What are you doing?'

'Setting your mind at ease,' he lied. 'I figured you would prefer to do this...*test* kiss in here, rather than on a bed. I don't know if I can trust you not to get too carried away.'

No need to tell her that he barely trusted himself not to get too carried away.

'Right,' she muttered huskily, not even realising that he hadn't tried to deny it.

He rather liked that. Just as liked the heat of her backside against the solid length of his sex. Making it more of a gratifying ache than a painful one.

'Now what?' she quipped. But the tremor in her voice gave her away, betraying her desire, just as he'd hoped.

Encouraging her to loop her arms around his neck, Lukas dipped his head to her, inhaling that fresh scent he remembered from the cathedral. It smelled more of tropical hair shampoo than any heavy, cloying perfume—only making her seem that much more innocent.

'Now what?' Her voice seemed to flutter around her, and he couldn't hold himself back any longer.

Bending his head, he didn't wait, he didn't warn. He just took.

Everything in Oti jolted, like grabbing hold of one of the electrified fences that had once been set up around their camp in Sudan.

Only far, far more pleasant.

Lukas was just as charged, just as stirring. And there had to be something seriously amiss with her because she revelled in every second of it.

The delicious crush of his mouth on hers, and the glorious sweep of that clever tongue.

Her arms were already around his neck, but now she used them to pull him closer, pressing her body tighter up against his, the feel of his hard length beneath her doing nothing to ease that heavy throb between her legs. And there was no way she could silence those giveaway sounds that were coming from her throat, of longing and of greed.

But, for his part, Lukas didn't appear any more controlled. His low growl of approval when she'd rocked over him had slid through her like honey. Warming her and spreading inside her. She tried it again, and this time he wrenched his mouth away from her.

'Be very careful,' he began, his voice so hoarse with desire that it made her breasts ache. 'I suggest you don't waken what you aren't prepared to deal with.'

And despite the fact that she had no real idea what she was doing, having never slept with any man before, Oti dropped her head to graze her teeth gently against the column of his neck.

'I'm more than prepared to deal with anything I awaken.'

He didn't hesitate. Dropping his head to reclaim her mouth, kissing her as thoroughly as if he were branding her, Lukas moved his attention to her jaw. Soft, butterfly-like kisses that had her murmuring softly, followed by a trail leading down her elegant neck and to her collarbone.

Oti couldn't help it. She became pliable and soft in his arms, moulding herself to him, just like she had in the cathedral, except this time, without an audience, she allowed her hands to roam freely over that sculpted chest, intent on exploring every inch of his incredible body and learning every ridge and every dip.

But it was getting harder and harder to concentrate when Lukas was tracing whorls on her skin like that as he moved. Until, at last, he reached the deep V neckline of her top. His mouth, his tongue, traced their way over her skin, the top of her chest, and dipped beneath the fabric.

And all she could think was how much more

she wanted. How badly she ached for him. She tried to tell him what she wanted—*needed*—but then, seeming to read her body like a glorious book, Lukas hooked his fingers under her top and lifted it over her head with an impressive economy of movement.

'You've practised that,' she tried to joke, something prodding her that she ought to be more wary about his sheer skill and efficiency.

But as she watched him fingering the delicate electric blue lace of her bra, something approaching marvel clouding his features, it was hard to even breathe, let alone talk.

'Stunning,' he growled.

And then he dispensed with that too, leaving her naked from the waist up, and feeling more feminine and wanton than she thought she'd ever felt before.

His eyes were almost black with the same desire that echoed within her. In all the places that no one had ever touched. Then they locked with hers as he cupped one of her breasts in his palm and she could only look on, transfixed, as he tested it, gloried in it and tasted it.

She had no idea what the sound was that came out of her mouth. Something primitive. Her body seemed to arch involuntarily, as if offering herself up to him all the more.

He feasted on her for a lifetime, maybe two,

before switching sides to repeat the entire process. As if he had all the time in the world. Nowhere else to ever be. Nothing else to ever do.

He treated her as if she were infinitely precious, and even though a voice in her head tried to remind her that it was all fake, she didn't care.

And then, with deliberate care and his eyes still holding hers, he rubbed one calloused thumb pad over her taut, tender nipple and a low sigh escaped her as her eyes drifted closed. She wasn't prepared for the wallop of sensation when his mouth suddenly closed over it, drawing it into his mouth, sucking it deeper and letting his teeth slide over it, then soothing it with his cool, wicked tongue.

It was entirely possible, and embarrassing, that she was going to come apart just at that, and Oti couldn't bring herself to care. It was too good.

Too right.

Never, in all her wildest dreams, had she thought this was how she and Lukas would end up.

The convenient reality of their situation splashed into her head like a douse of cold water.

Lukas lifted his head up instantly. 'What is it?'

She'd almost forgotten when she'd started this…or agreed to it? Oti couldn't quite remember how it had begun; Lukas had her so twisted inside out with pleasure.

But the fact was that she'd called her father as

soon as she'd left Edward, asking for her share of the money he'd extorted from Lukas.

He'd laughed callously at her before hanging up. Reneging on his promise, just as she'd always feared he would.

Begging Lukas for the money for Edward's surgery was now her only chance. Getting caught up in his kisses and forgetting the endgame certainly wasn't part of her plan.

'I have to ask you...' She faltered.

It was crazy how much she wanted to swallow the words down, stuff them away and simply enjoy this one night with Lukas. To let him show her what she'd been saving herself for all these years.

But Edward and his needs were supposed to be the entire reason she had gone through with this charade. With everything that her brother had put up with these past few years, was she really selfish enough to put a few hours of carnal lust ahead of what might save Edward's life?

Struggling to a more upright position, acutely aware that she was naked from the waist up, Oti kept her arms around Lukas's neck, as if that could somehow afford her a little dignity.

What if she told him the truth? Maybe she could appeal to his sense of decency. He certainly had some—more than she'd initially given him credit for, and certainly more than her father had ever had.

But what if he used it as leverage against her, just as her own father had done? Could she really trust a man she barely knew, just because he made her body come alive in a way that she hadn't known it was capable of doing?

'What is it, Octavia?' Lukas demanded, and his concern only added to her guilt.

'I need to ask you a favour,' she began, flicking out her tongue in a fruitless effort to moisten her suddenly dry lips.

Beneath her, Lukas had grown still, tense, his hooded eyes disguising his reaction from her. But she forced herself to carry on.

'Like you said, consummation wasn't part of the deal you made with my father.'

'The deal?' Lukas echoed, and she knew she didn't imagine the mounting fury in his tone.

Still, she pressed on. For Edward.

'Yes, the deal. You got my brother's company, my father got money and he got to wash his hands of me. But now it's my turn.'

'Your turn?'

There was no doubting his expression of disgust. Unlinking her hands from around him, he thrust her away and onto the couch, hardly able to get away from her any faster.

'I want to come out of this with something too.'

'Is that what this was all about?' he spat out. 'Money?'

'No,' she cried instinctively, before realising her mistake. 'Yes, but…for a good reason.'

Misery racked her.

'Save it, Octavia.' His voice was harsh, and it seemed to claw at her from the inside out. 'You really are your father's daughter now. Save the excuses, however. I don't want to hear them. How much?'

'Lukas…please…'

'How much?' he repeated, and she didn't dare argue again.

She named a sum that she knew would cover the cost of the operation, not a penny more, and couldn't stop herself from lamenting the fact that if her father had shared the pot he'd extorted from Lukas she wouldn't have to be asking for this now.

'You will have your money…'

'Lukas, please know that…'

'The money will be there,' he bit out. 'You don't need to whore yourself out for it.'

And then, before she could say anything else—even if she'd had a clue what to say—he had stalked across the room and into his own suite, the unmistakable sound of the key turning in the lock making it clear that he was rejecting her.

She could hardly blame him. But it didn't stop her from throwing herself onto the huge marshmallow pillows of her bed and sobbing herself to sleep.

Yet what choice did she have?

The day could hardly have gone much worse. And it was all her own doing.

CHAPTER SIX

SINKING BACK INTO the creamy soft seats of the limousine, Oti fought the urge to close her eyes.

She hadn't slept a wink for the last couple of days, tossing and turning each night, her thoughts returning over and over to Lukas. And that kiss.

The way her whole body ignited each time she replayed it in her head. No one had ever come close to making her feel like Lukas did. Making her ache like he did.

After what had happened to her that ghastly night almost fifteen years ago, she'd begun to think that no one ever would.

In fact, she'd begun to conclude that there had to be something wrong with her. Why had she insisted on carrying it with her, letting it over-shadow any hint of a relationship with any man since?

Ultimately, she'd been rescued. Other women went through far, far worse ordeals. So why had she carried it with her all these years? Why didn't she feel the same drive that other young women her age felt?

And then Lukas had stepped into her life and she'd felt something shift inside her, even from their first meeting. However much she'd tried to pretend otherwise, there had been something about Lukas that had simply lifted all those heavy, suffocating layers away.

She'd thought their kiss in the cathedral had been unbalancing enough, but the other night had just upended her world completely.

Oti couldn't stop replaying it. It was on a loop that she couldn't—didn't want to—break. And that made the man so much more dangerous to her. Just like she'd always thought he was.

God, how she'd wanted him to keep kissing her. To touch her, the way he'd deliciously threatened to do. That rich, dark voice of his had played with her senses, turning them in on themselves so that she could barely think straight.

So that all she'd been able to think of was Lukas, and the way he'd been tasting her. Teasing her. She'd felt so wanton—desired and desirable. More than that, he'd made her feel as if there was nothing lacking about her at all. As if she'd just been waiting for this—for *him*—all this time. It was surely one of Lukas's greatest skills, and she'd been helpless to resist him.

If he hadn't stopped, then Oti was in no doubt

that she would have given herself up to him right there and then, on that sofa in her bedroom suite.

Giving her virginity to a man who barely liked her, let alone loved her.

She might ask herself what she'd been thinking, except the truth of it was that she hadn't been *thinking*. She hadn't been capable of thinking at all.

Edward was right. She'd been playing with fire the moment she'd agreed to her father's preposterous plan to marry her off to a man like Lukas Woods. Whilst she might have told herself that she was sacrificing herself for a greater purpose—to get money for Edward's surgery—the truth was far less noble.

She had wanted Lukas from that very first meeting, in a terrifyingly exciting, utterly carnal way. Her body had recognised it, even if her mind had refused to accept it.

But it was getting harder and harder to lie to herself. Not least because the money was there—from Lukas—in her account, and still…that raw, urgent longing hadn't gone away.

It was all so confusing.

The fact that she hadn't even had to sleep with the man told her so much more about what kind of a person he was. And it didn't match the ruthlessness of his reputation.

She should have everything she wanted. And yet she didn't. Because what a part of her really seemed to want—physically if not emotionally, of course; she wasn't that crazy—was Lukas. And she couldn't shake that sense of regret and blame over what had happened between them the other night.

Nor the rawness that scraped somewhere unfathomable, deep inside her chest.

Perhaps talking to Edward again today would clear that up. Being able to finally assure him that the procedure was a possibility—that, as long as the tests proved him to be a viable candidate, money wouldn't be a stumbling block—should erase any lingering doubts about Lukas from her mind.

As well as any final remnants of guilt.

'Commandeering my driver again?'

For the third time in almost as many days, Oti found herself startled by her fake husband. She watched, horrified, as he slid into the back seat across from her. She tried—and failed—to stop her eyes from soaking up the sight of his long, mouth-wateringly muscular legs, which his tailored suit did nothing to diminish. Quite the contrary; they stretched out in front of him so very languidly, practically inviting her gaze to roam upward.

Oti blew out a breath of frustration. Even here, in the back seat of a car, he wore power like a bespoke suit. And, like everything else, it fitted him immaculately.

'What are you doing, Lukas?' she managed, her voice scratchier than she would have liked. But that couldn't be helped.

'Heading into the office. Some of us work for a living.'

She bit her lip to stop herself from answering. There was no need to tell him about her job—it didn't matter to her at all what he thought.

If only she could believe that.

'You aren't driving yourself? Only you have done the last few days.'

'You haven't used my driver the last few days,' he pointed out.

'So you're only here because I am?' She could hardly matter that much to him, surely?

'After last time, can you blame me?'

Shame and anger bled into each other and Oti opened her mouth to answer, only for the driver to alert them to an accident further up the road.

'The report says that traffic is gridlocked, sir,' George, the driver, continued. 'We could go the longer way around—the roads that way are quieter.'

'Do that,' Lukas confirmed as Oti's heart lurched.

A longer car ride, with the tension already palpable? Just what she didn't need.

The car turned and they drove in silence for a while and Oti forced herself to stare out of the window. Anything not to have to engage with him.

More because she feared confusion and—shamefully—lust would be written all over her features.

It was only as they pulled up at a set of red lights that Oti found her gaze pulled to the commotion going on in a car parked awkwardly in the kerb, though it took her a few moments to work out exactly what she was seeing.

'Stop the car!' she yelled, just as George began to pull away again.

It vaguely registered that it took Lukas repeating the instruction for the driver to obey.

'What's going on?' His voice was low, almost guarded.

'Unlock the doors, George. *Now.* I think the woman in that car is in labour, and she's on her own.'

The door clicked and she practically stumbled out as she hurried back to the other car, only realising that Lukas was right alongside her as she reached the passenger side.

'George is calling an ambulance,' he told her quickly. 'I don't think it's wise to interfere. Leave it to the professionals when they arrive.'

Oti didn't reply; she just picked up her pace. Tapping on the car window, she then stepped back to give the grunting woman space.

'I'm Oti, I'm a doctor. I'm here to help.'

With another grunt and a twisted expression, the woman managed to unlock the car door, and Oti hauled it open.

'My husband...' the woman managed between groans. 'He forgot his mobile in the panic to leave the house. He...he ran to the petrol station down the road with our son to...make the call.'

'Okay, so is this your second baby?' Oti asked. 'Can you tell me your name?'

'Debi... This is my...second. Yes... I was...in labour for ten hours with him... This one can't come...yet.'

'Yeah, it happens that way sometimes.' Oti offered a gentle laugh. 'Hours for the first, but the second is quick. Nothing to worry about. I can tell your contractions aren't far apart at all. Can we get you into the back seat so there's a little more room for me to examine you?'

She felt Lukas's hand at her elbow, drawing her away.

'You need to wait for the professionals,' he ground out in a low voice.

'I'm a doctor,' she reminded him irritably, beginning to wrench her arm away.

His grip tightened.

'You might have bought your degree,' he hissed, 'but that doesn't make you a practising doctor. You can't play superhero with this woman's baby.'

Oti had had enough. Never mind her own sense of privacy or keeping her secrets. This woman needed her, and she wasn't about to let Lukas stop her from doing the one thing she did best.

'For pity's sake, Lukas, I *am* a professional,' she hissed up at him. 'I haven't been on the beach, or whatever my father has claimed. I've been working in South Sudan for the past four years, looking after women and children, including delivering babies. On an average day, our small unit can help deliver sixty babies in a twenty-four-hour period. I know what I'm doing.'

Later, she would savour that stunned expression which passed over his face. The way he stopped looking at her with quite such a mixture of pity and disdain. The moment he began to see her in a different light.

Later.

But right now she had a job to do.

'Get the first aid kit from your limo—your driver will know where it is if you don't. I need gloves, and hand sanitizer if there is any.'

She occupied herself with helping Debi from the passenger seat to the back seat, settling the woman into position just as Lukas returned with the gloves and gel.

'Okay, Debi, it's going to be okay. I just need to check how dilated you are, and see if I can feel the baby's head.'

'The ambulance is on its way,' Lukas murmured just before Oti moved back to her patient.

'But that accident we were avoiding is blocking the road for everyone.'

'Understood.' She nodded, stepping away from him. 'Okay, Debi, let's see how you're doing.'

She dropped down to begin her check, but even in that instant her suspicions were confirmed. Still, she took a moment to confirm all was okay before pasting a bright smile on her face as she stood up.

'Okay, so you're fully dilated, Debi, and I can see the baby's head. Your baby is clearly eager to meet you, so I don't think we're going to be able to wait until the ambulance arrives.'

'I can't deliver here,' Debi gasped. 'In the back seat of the car, in the middle of the road.'

'It happens more often than you might think,' Oti soothed, turning quickly to Lukas. 'Can you get me water, paper towels or something like it, and scissors?'

Then she glanced him up and down, her eyes alighting on his suit footwear.

'And give me your shoelaces.'

His curt nod before swinging around to obey her gave Oti a ridiculous kick of pleasure. As though something had *shifted* between them. In a good way. She thrust it aside, focusing on her patient instead and busying herself with keeping Debi calm, and breathing properly.

But the birth was happening fast.

Crouching down on the ground, she watched the baby as she heard her patient give a more guttural grunt. There was nothing else for it.

'Push,' Oti ordered. *'Push.'*

With a loud cry, the woman pushed, and the baby slithered straight out and into Oti's arms, and all she could do was pray that she didn't drop it.

'Scissors, water, paper towels, and the rug from the car.' Lukas's voice came from behind her as she swung around to face him. 'Oh.'

He stopped abruptly, gazing in horror at the baby in her arms. It might have been comical under any other circumstances. To see the all-powerful, always controlled Lukas Woods look so thrown.

'Lay the paper towels on the seat,' she instructed. 'Quickly.'

To his credit, he gathered himself instantly, laying them down so that Oti was able to clean and massage the baby until she heard that first beautiful cry.

'Shoelaces and scissors?' She turned to Lukas as he was just standing up from untying them.

Wordlessly, he handed her both and, conscious that his eyes were still on her, she busied herself with tying off the umbilical cord and then cutting it. Finally, wrapping the baby up warmly,

Oti handed the precious bundle to an emotional but happy mother.

'Meet your daughter—ten fingers, ten toes and a healthy set of lungs.'

'My husband...?'

'I'll head up the road to look for him.' Lukas didn't hesitate. 'Let him know what's happened.'

And as he left Oti was almost grateful for the space. It was a chance to decompress. This time, she was in no doubt that Lukas would have questions but, far from dreading them as she might have a week ago, she thought she might actually welcome them.

It would be a chance to let Lukas see the real her and maybe erase some of the less than flattering opinion he had of her as some dumb socialite.

And even though she knew it should worry her that his opinion of her mattered so much, Oti couldn't seem to escape the notion.

She was still fighting her own thoughts when Lukas returned with the rather frantic-looking husband and the couple's relatively nonplussed son in tow. Keeping their distance, the two of them tried to give the family space as they all waited for the ambulance.

'You should have told me,' Lukas bit out eventually.

Oti paused in the process of shoving the bloodied paper towels into the bin-liner, though she deliberately didn't look at him. She didn't need to ask what he was talking about.

'Would you have believed me?' she asked quietly.

'I'd have had it looked into.'

The saddest part, Oti thought, was that he actually thought she would find that reassuring.

'So you wouldn't have believed me,' she pointed out. 'You wouldn't have taken my word for it.'

He actually hesitated. The man renowned for never missing a beat. It felt like a small victory, even as she chastened herself for caring about that.

'Why would you let people paint you as some vacuous, party-hard It-girl who's permanently living it up on some extended tropical holiday? Or that you're in rehab yet again?'

She tilted her head up to him. 'What difference does it make?'

'What difference?' he echoed, appalled. 'Look at what you just did. That was...*incredible*.'

He shook his head as though he couldn't actually find the words and, even though Oti tried to pretend his words didn't affect her, there was no denying that ball of pride which swelled inside her, just hearing the admiration in his tone.

Lukas Woods thought she was *incredible*.

'What could you possibly gain by not telling anyone the truth?' he demanded angrily.

Oti didn't know how, but she managed a shrug.

'The truth gets distorted by what people want to see.'

'All the more reason to tell them.'

'They wouldn't have wanted to hear it,' she countered evenly.

'Then you make them.'

'Why? What does their opinion matter to me?' She even let a laugh escape her, a genuine one. Because her next observation, at least, was true. 'You certainly don't let yourself get affected by what other people think.'

'They don't think I'm a party girl.'

'But *I* know I'm not. And besides, they think you're a ruthless playboy. But you aren't really, are you?'

He didn't answer, but the glare that he shot at her might have skewered a lesser woman. Right now, though, she felt anything but *lesser*.

'You really don't care what people think, do you?' His eyes seemed to root her to the spot.

She couldn't move. She wasn't even sure she could breathe.

It was as though Lukas was seeing her for the first time. Or, if not that, then certainly through fresh eyes. And she found the whole experience almost exhilarating.

'You're not at all the girl I thought.'

'Well, then——' she wasn't entirely sure how she managed to sound so breezy '—it serves you right for not doing your homework on me properly, doesn't it? I can't imagine you're usually so lax when it comes to business. I can only take it as further proof that you aren't as cold-blooded as you like people to believe.'

'In fact,' he continued as if she hadn't spoken, 'you're not a *girl* at all, are you?'

And, before she could answer, he reached out and took a lock of her hair, rolling it between his thumb and forefinger for a moment, before tucking it behind her ear.

It was such a soft, unexpected, *intimate* gesture. And it wiped all thought from Oti's mind.

But then he simply took the rubbish bag from her, stalking to the public bin on the pavement and dropped their rubbish in the slot which would take it to the underground storage.

Then he paced back to her, before turning to sit on the bonnet of the limo, his legs stretched in their usual position, his arms folded across his chest, highlighting his chest and biceps. Not a close-cut hair out of place. The trousers and waistcoat of his bespoke suit as immaculate as usual on his sculpted frame.

And Oti watched his every movement as though beguiled. A billionaire who was accustomed to snapping his fingers and everyone leaping to attention, yet he hadn't been too proud to help her with the baby, and the clean-up afterwards. A man who wasn't afraid of getting his hands dirty—quite literally.

Despite all her caution, the more time she spent with Lukas, the more she found herself admiring him. Respecting him. And having that respect reflected back at her now when he looked at her was…exhilarating.

Yet it was also terrifying. Because, if she wasn't careful, she could end up confusing attraction and respect, could end up falling for the man. A man who didn't remotely feel the same way about her.

She eyed the horizon as a hundred—a thousand—thoughts crashed around her head. But there were so many of them and they were all so intertwined that she had no idea where to even begin unravelling the truth. And at the centre of it was that one single event that she didn't want to have to talk about to anyone.

Certainly not to Lukas.

'Then why did your father perpetuate those rumours?' Lukas demanded after a while.

'Because he doesn't know the truth.'

'You can't expect me to believe that, surely?'

'My father hasn't noticed me since I was *that* girl, all those years ago. He's a selfish and self-serving man, but I think you already know that.'

'I do indeed. So surely he would have preferred to use your success as a doctor to somehow turn it around to his own success as a father?'

'He would have, yes,' she agreed evenly. 'Which is why I never told him. I suppose I thought he'd work it out eventually. The fact that he never has speaks for itself, I think.'

'So he would rather paint you as an addict who wastes her life partying abroad, and ends up in rehab all too often?' Lukas's disdain was unmistakable, and Oti felt her mouth twist into a hollow smile.

'Ironically, that helps him.'

'I fail to see how.'

'That's because you aren't like my father.' Her gaze was drawn to Lukas despite herself, and her smile became a little less hollow and a little warmer. 'That's a compliment.'

'Indeed it is,' he answered grimly.

'You may be calculating and ruthless when it comes to work, but you aren't nearly as intrusive when it comes to more personal matters.' She smiled. 'You're a nicer person than you want the world to see. I just don't understand why.'

'And again—' Lukas arched an eyebrow at her, making her hands actually itch to reach out and smooth it '—this isn't about me.'

'Perhaps I'm hoping that if I open up to you then you might afford me the same courtesy.'

She didn't realise how true that was until she heard the words come out of her mouth.

'Don't bank on it,' he growled softly.

But it lacked any bite and Oti felt her smile warming her from the inside. She dipped her head to conceal it.

'Fair enough. Either way, my point is that it suited my father to let people think I was still that wild child. Whilst they were speculating about me, they weren't looking at him. Plus, there were rumours that he was having some financial trouble, and I became the perfect scapegoat.'

'He could tell them that you had blown through your inheritance on exotic holidays, wild parties and drugs,' Lukas realised. 'That way, no one would think he was the one who'd lost it all gambling.'

'He could also claim that he'd spent hundreds of thousands sending me to rehab.'

'The man's a degenerate,' Lukas snarled. 'But you're a fool for letting him get away with painting you that way. Why wouldn't you say something?'

She could tell him about HOP, and how she'd always feared her father would piggyback onto the charity and try to use her involvement with it to somehow improve his image. And then she thought about Edward, and how his accident was the reason that she'd ended up fleeing to the charity in the first instance.

She couldn't tell Lukas about one without the other.

'It's complicated,' she hedged at last.

'And that's a cop-out.'

His look of disappointment cut through her, but the distant wail of an ambulance siren saved her from the need to answer. They each lapsed into silence, waiting for the sound to get closer, as Oti tried to pretend to herself that she didn't care that Lukas had been so easily stopped from asking her anything more.

And yet she waited and held her breath. But he still didn't speak. She needed to pull herself together.

'I'd better go and alert my new patient,' she commented, standing up straight. 'They look like they're all too preoccupied to have heard it.'

'Will you need to accompany them to the hospital?' Lukas asked.

'I don't think so.' She shook her head. 'There were no complications, so a handover to the paramedics should suffice.'

'Good. Then we'll head back home and talk properly.'

'No, I can't...' The words came out in a panicked rush. 'I have to go and see... I have to go.'

She could feel the change in Lukas instantly. Even if she hadn't been so close that she could feel him tense, she would have felt it in the way the air around them tightened. It thickened.

'That will not happen, Octavia. You're not going anywhere until we've talked.'

'I don't know what you think is going on here,' Oti cried desperately. 'But I have to go. I need to see Edward.'

'Edward?'

'My brother.' She watched Lukas's expression change from anger to disbelief to shock, all in the space of about a second, and it occurred to her that she was far too tuned in to the man if she could recognise all that so easily. 'The money I needed from you was for him. For an operation.'

'I thought your brother died,' he said slowly.

'He didn't.' Misery washed over her at the disgust beginning to settle over Lukas's features. 'That was another of my father's lies.'

And one that Edward had wanted her repeat, if only for his own dignity. But she wasn't about to tell Lukas that.

The sirens' wail was louder now, and Oti knew she had to go. But she felt rooted to the spot. Paralysed.

'Go and help your patient. I'll leave George to take you to Edward.'

'You're going?' She didn't know why she felt so surprised. Or so deflated.

'I have a meeting to get to.'

There really was no reason for her to feel disappointed. So why did she?

'Then take the car, Lukas.'

He pushed himself off the bonnet and began to move away.

'I'll walk.' His tone was inscrutable. 'I need to think, anyway, and the fresh air will do me good.'

He stepped around the car and reached inside to retrieve his phone and jacket, slinging it over his shoulder as he walked away. Try as she might, she couldn't seem to drag her eyes from him.

'And what then?' she asked thickly.

Lukas turned to look at her, the expression in his eyes almost ominous.

'Then, Octavia, you are going to come home, and you are going to tell me everything.'

And it struck Oti as more than a little telling that the part her unguarded heart clung on to most tightly in that instruction was when he told her to *come home*.

CHAPTER SEVEN

OCTAVIA WAS IN his sleek living room, already waiting for him, when Lukas finally arrived home that evening.

She looked serene and composed, and utterly in control—just as she had done that morning helping the mother give birth to her child inside that car. As though this was the kind of thing she did every day.

He suspected, from all the research he had spent the day doing, including her charity work with Health Overseas Project, that it wasn't too far from the truth.

Octavia—or Oti, as she preferred to be called—wasn't at all the woman that he'd believed her to be.

Had he ever been so mistaken about someone?

The question had been running through his head for the past several hours, though he knew the answer of course. It was because that was all he'd been expecting her to be. It was all that he'd *wanted* her to be.

He'd known her reputation didn't fit from practically the first moment they'd met, when she'd sent all his senses into full alert. But he'd ignored it because it hadn't suited the narrative he'd wanted to write.

Then he'd realised it again in the cathedral, when she'd stood in front of him and he'd felt as if his skull was cracking with the effort of resisting her. And he'd certainly realised it on witnessing the way she'd taken charge during Andrew Rockman's heart attack. But he'd ignored it on those occasions too, because he'd been so focused on stealing Sedeshire International out from under Rockman's nose. And he'd been using her to finally trounce that man, once and for all.

Now, though, it was time to face up to the fact that he should never have married her. Oti deserved better than to be a pawn in such a game, and he should have known that.

Lukas crossed the room to pour himself a drink from the cabinet—more for something to do than because he actually wanted one—and then took out a glass for her.

'I take it you do drink?' he asked brusquely. 'Given that you're clearly not in need of any twelve-step programme after all.'

He hadn't intended to sound quite so abrasive and, in any case, his anger was directed more at himself than at Oti. But he wasn't accustomed to missing things, certainly not in business. Oti might believe it showed he wasn't quite as ruthless as he liked to appear, and it was ridiculous how much Lukas wanted to be the man she thought he was. However, he suspected the truth was far less selfless.

The simple fact was that whilst business was always clear and easy for him, marrying Oti had been about furthering his revenge for his mother. He had nearly—finally—succeeded in the plan he'd formulated back when he'd been a twelve-year-old kid. A plan he'd tweaked slightly over the years, but which had essentially stayed the same.

A plan which he'd been impatient to execute because he'd wanted to move on with his life. Truth be told, he'd wanted it over with a decade ago. But he couldn't simply abandon it—he couldn't simply let his mother's death go without exacting some sort of punishment.

'I do drink, yes.' Oti's quiet voice dragged him mercifully back to the present. 'Though I prefer wine to brandy.'

'Red or white?'

'Red, if there's a choice,' she replied, unfailingly polite, which nearly killed him.

He opened the bespoke wine cabinet and selected a bottle, then set about opening it. In silence again, feigning a patience that he didn't feel, until at last he was crossing the room towards her and setting the glass of wine down on the expensive coffee table.

'Thank you,' she murmured, lifting the glass elegantly and taking a sip before setting it back down.

He wasn't sure why, but he wondered if she found it as tasteless as he currently found his favourite brandy.

Moving away, Lukas found himself at the huge picture window. The view had always made him feel as though the city—and what felt like the entire world—was at his feet, but now Lukas peered down the long, straight, wide roads as if seeing past the city's boundaries would somehow let him see the big picture that he'd been missing all this time.

'Ask me what you want to know, Lukas.' Her quiet voice flowed over him.

He didn't turn around.

'How about we start with why you went along with your father's sick story that your brother was dead?'

His choice of words was designed to twist into her, too barbed to go unnoticed. Yet it didn't escape him that he deliberately kept his back to her so that he didn't have to see the expression in her eyes. So it surprised him when her tone stayed even.

'I didn't go along with my father's sick story.'

He turned despite himself.

'It was Edward's request,' she continued smoothly. 'It just happened to have the same result as my father intended.'

'*Edward* asked you to say he was dead?' Lukas asked, wholly unprepared for the look of pain that crossed her delicate features before she seemed to steel herself.

And in that instant he hated that she had to wear such a mask around him.

'My brother told me on multiple occasions that he wanted to…die.'

Lukas didn't answer, not having a clue what to even begin to say.

'The crash was bad.'

'I saw the news reports at the time,' Lukas confirmed.

Not to mention the fact that he'd done an internet search that afternoon, unable to concentrate on his meeting. Or any of the work that demanded his attention, for that matter.

It had been late on Christmas Eve, and Edward had allegedly been driving on a narrow, unlit valley road in the driving rain when an oncoming driver had lost control and skidded around the bend on Edward's side of the road.

His vehicle had been rammed through the drystone wall and who knew how many times it had tumbled down the steep rocky slope before coming to a halt at the bottom, on its roof.

When had he crossed the room again? When had he lowered himself into the chair opposite her?

'His injuries were...*are* significant.'

'But he's alive,' Lukas clarified. 'Is he in a coma?'

'No, he isn't.'

He didn't particularly appreciate the feeling creeping through him at that moment.

'He has brain damage?'

'No, he's alert, and his mind is as sharp as it ever was.'

'I just bought the controlling shares of his company.' Lukas eyed her grimly. He'd never regretted a business deal in his life. Until now.

'Edward's well aware.' Her expression was rueful. 'But, as far as he's concerned, it's better in your hands than Rockman's.'

'If his mind is still sharp, then why not keep the company? I only met him a couple of times, but he always struck me as a good CEO.'

'He was. Most of the board agreed,' she told him in a voice that Lukas now recognised was too calm, too controlled. As if she had a tight lid on myriad emotions which bubbled within but couldn't afford to let a single one of them show. 'Sadly, a few didn't, and Edward agreed.'

She stopped abruptly. Lukas could have asked more, but he wanted her to tell him when she was ready. Clamping his jaw shut, he forced himself to wait.

'He's tetraplegic,' she announced after what felt like an age. 'He's stuck in a wheelchair, he can't move his arms or legs, he can't even grasp things, and as far as Edward is concerned it's no life at all.'

'Yet, asking you to pretend he was dead—' Lukas shook his head '—isn't that a bit extreme?'

'Not if he wanted to protect his privacy. His dignity.' She shook her head. 'He was an amateur racing car enthusiast, Lukas. The media were seriously attracted to him. Almost as much as you. Can you imagine if you were in an accident? The lengths they would go to get to you? In the first few days alone, after Edward's accident, we caught three reporters or photographers dressed up as hospital porters, or a nurse, just to get in and get a photo of him. One of them even succeeded.'

He remembered it in that instant, the image flashing into his mind, making him wonder how he'd forgotten it. He'd been hooked up to machines and surrounded by tubes and wires. If it were himself, he could see how it would unnerve the board at LVW Industries.

'So the photo of him in a coma, four years ago, wasn't released by the family, as was claimed?' Lukas realised with a jolt.

'No, it was not. Not even my father would admit to Edward's condition, even for money.'

This was what Oti had gone through? Having to deal with a relentless press whilst trying to come to terms with the seriousness of her brother's accident. Especially after losing her mother six years earlier.

'We had him moved to a private, very discreet medical facility. Fortunately, as company founder, he had the highest level of medical cover. Plus, the board wanted to keep the extent of his injuries concealed until they knew more, so as not to frighten any shareholders. Which was fortunate, since I can't imagine my father had the means or the inclination to pay for Edward's treatment.'

Neither could Lukas, but he wisely stayed silent.

'At first, all I prayed for was that he would wake up. Then, when he couldn't feel anything, I prayed that it was just bruising. We kept hoping that once the swelling went down he would be okay, albeit with rehabilitation. By the time we realised the full extent of his injuries, Edward had decided that he didn't want anyone to know until he had come to terms with it himself, and the board agreed. It was decided that, as the press would be relentless in trying to get a photo of him as long as they knew he was alive, it was easier to pretend otherwise.'

'And your father?'

'He was only too happy to wash his hands of a son with a disability.' Finally, she couldn't keep the bitterness from her tone.

She looked so broken and defeated, so unlike the woman he'd imagined she was. And suddenly all Lukas wanted to do was go to her, scoop her into his arms and take all her pain away.

He had no idea where that came from.

Not least because he never allowed himself to feel anything. It made no sense.

'Is that why you started volunteering in South Sudan?'

'I wouldn't have, if Edward hadn't banned me from even visiting him for the first two years.' She jerked her head up, her tone defensive.

'I wasn't attacking you.'

She eyed him warily, and he found he didn't much like that either.

'I had to get away. I needed to do something meaningful. And, although I'd managed to drop off the media's radar for years, without Edward to pursue any more, they turned their attention back to me.'

'I believe there were articles,' he mused, 'and photos of wild parties and reckless behaviour.'

'Old photos that hadn't been released before.' She looked embarrassed nonetheless. 'I suspect people released them for money. Maybe even my father. And I could have fought them, but what would have been the point? People only want the salacious story. The pictures were of me—no one really cared whether they were out of date or not. Besides, I earned my wild-child reputation by my own actions.'

There was such a bleak turn to her countenance that it scraped at something inside Lukas. He couldn't have said why he suspected there was far more to the story. Nor could he explain how he knew that now wasn't the time to press her on it. So instead he asked her something else.

'You said the money I gave you is for Edward?'

'There's an operation.' She scrunched up her face and he got the impression that she was trying to decide how best to explain it.

He, a man who usually had to explain the intricate workings of computer programming or robotic workings to others. It might have been amusing, under other circumstances.

'There's a new operation. A combined nerve and tendon transfer, which could help him. Possibly. There's no guarantee. It's in clinical trials.'

'So he's in a trial?'

'No, the nature of his injuries mean that he isn't eligible for the trials. But we can still pay privately. I just didn't have a way of guaranteeing the money and so I couldn't even get him to agree to have an assessment to see if he would be a good candidate.'

'And now you have my money.'

'I won't apologise, Lukas.' She glowered.

'I don't expect you to. I'm assuring you that, no matter what else happens, you have my money. *Your* money. Whatever your brother needs, come to me. It's just money, Oti.'

Shock then relief skittered over her lovely face. And then she smiled and her face lit up. It was like being dazzled by the light from the glory of the sun itself.

More than that, it seemed to warm his very soul. It seemed to make it feel whole again.

'I called them today and they'll see him at the end of the week.' She shifted in her chair and he realised it was with excitement.

And something else that he couldn't quite isolate. As much as he didn't want to dampen her mood, Lukas couldn't help asking more questions.

'Do you mean that?' She sounded almost breathless, and what did it say about him that he liked the impact he'd had on her?

'I do. So your father wouldn't pay for any of it?' he asked.

'He said he would. He promised he would pay for it with the obscene sum he extorted from you. But…' She trailed off.

'That's why you agreed to marry me,' Lukas realised. 'Your father promised to pay for Edward's operation if you married me.'

'Yes.'

'He reneged, though. That's why you asked me. As your husband, I'd be honour-bound to agree? It was a last resort, but you still thought I needed buttering up?'

He didn't need to spell it out for her; she was clearly embarrassed enough. She was also torn. He could read it in every line of her tense body. Still, he wasn't surprised when she tried to defend the repugnant man.

'I hoped he would honour it.'

'Your father is too greedy for honour, Oti,' Lukas murmured quietly. 'He wanted the money for himself, whilst you wanted the money to save your brother's life.'

'You make it sound entirely noble and self-less.' She frowned.

'Because it is.' Remorse stirred within him. 'You're the only one who hasn't been self-serving throughout this entire arrangement.'

'Am I?' Her gaze slammed into his without warning. 'So why *did* you marry me, Lukas? What's in it for you? I mean, I understand the part of the deal where you got Edward's company, and my father got his money, but why me?'

It was on the tip of his tongue to tell her that this conversation was about her, not him—just as he had back at the roadside that morning—but the words didn't come.

'I'm guessing my father thought our marriage might somehow keep you around to tap for more money when he blows through the first lot. But why agree, Lukas? You could have refused that part of the deal. He would still have taken your deal—it was almost double anything Rockman could offer.'

What was it about this one unique woman that had him twisting and turning, no longer sure of the difference between black and white, night and day? It was all a glorious confusion where Oti was concerned.

And, for the first time, he felt an inexplicable urge to talk to her as he'd never talked to anyone in his life.

Oti wasn't sure at what point she realised she was holding her breath, but suddenly she was aware of the feeling that her lungs were about to burst.

Lukas had been silent for so long that it seemed as though he was actually going to talk to her. She desperately wanted him to. What wouldn't she give to be the person Lukas Woods talked to? In a way she seriously doubted the notoriously closed-off man had ever talked to anyone.

But then, without warning, he shut down again.

'You should have told me what was going on, Oti. I asked you several times if you knew what you were doing.'

'I remember.' She drew in a long breath, trying not to let the disappointment flood through her. 'And in that sense, yes, I knew. But I couldn't tell you about Edward, I didn't know what you would do—if you would use it as further lever-age against me.'

'You think I'm capable of that?'

He looked utterly appalled. But there was something adding to her disappointment now. Something more. Something like the beginnings of anger.

He wouldn't answer a single one of her ques-tions, yet he was virtually flaying her with every one of his. And she was supposed to answer with-out complaint?

'Yes. No. I don't know.' She exhaled her con-fusion. 'I thought so…but the more I've got to know you…'

And yet if the emergency this morning hadn't happened, she couldn't be sure that she would have said anything.

'How did you even get to be a doctor without everyone knowing?' He caught her by surprise.

'It's a long story.'

This was verging into territory that she didn't want to go.

'We have all night,' he answered evenly, but there was an unmistakable steel to his tone.

'It isn't that interesting.'

'It is to me,' he refuted.

'As is your life to me.' She didn't know where it came from, but she heard the words spilling out. 'Yet you keep all your secrets whilst demanding all of mine.'

He scowled at her, but he didn't refute what she said. Oti took that as progress.

'Tell me something about you, Lukas. Something no one else knows.'

The room fell quiet. Almost deafeningly silent. And even though she knew he wouldn't answer her, she couldn't bring herself to break it. She didn't want to be the one to speak first.

'Something like what?' he gritted out, taking her by surprise.

It took her a moment to regroup, her heart knocking around her chest as her mind rapidly sifted through the hundreds of questions that had flitted across her brain at once.

'Tell me about your parents,' she asked abruptly.

'My parents are dead, but you know that. I think the world knows I wrote my first app aged fifteen in the bedroom of my foster home.'

'A two-metre by one-metre cupboard that barely passed as a bedroom,' she couldn't help herself from saying. 'Yes, I've read that, but...'

'The size of the room was irrelevant.' He cut her off unexpectedly. 'It was my room. All mine. And the family left me in peace. I got shunted between multiple foster homes and care homes in the four years between my mother dying and my reaching sixteen, and that foster home was the only one where I felt safe. Secure.'

'I never knew that.'

And, deep down, she'd never expected Lukas to share anything real with her.

'No, well, the media prefer the lonely orphan story.' His tone was impartial. As though he hadn't told her something so personal. 'And I let them use that line because it kept the press away from the foster family's door, which has made it safer for other foster kids in care.'

There was something about his choice of language that caught her attention.

'Has made?' she queried. 'As in, you're still in touch with them?'

That definitely wasn't widely known. Lukas narrowed his eyes at her, giving her the sense that he was weighing her up.

'I hear from them occasionally. And I call from time to time. They're in their eighties now.'

'I didn't know.' She shook her head.

'Why would you?'

The air grew heavy and expectant again, until Oti was sure she could hear the very hair growing on her head. He'd already told her such a lot—far more than anything she'd ever read on the internet or in magazines over the years— and yet she couldn't seem to let the conversation end. She was suddenly hungry to know more, to understand better, and the voraciousness of her appetite should have terrified her.

'But before the foster home?' she began. 'Before your mother died?'

He didn't answer and, after a moment, she felt compelled to fill the silence.

'I'd just turned nineteen when my mother died. It was her death that shook me out of acting the wild child and made me realise I wanted to do something more with my life. That was when I went back to school, sat my A-levels and got myself into med school.'

'Is that why you let your father keep pretending that you were the out-of-control social-climber?' he asked almost offhandedly. 'Because you felt guilty that you hadn't got yourself together *before* your mother's death?'

Oti pursed her lips and let her eyes slide from Lukas. She'd never thought of it that way, and she didn't like what she heard. At the same time, it irked her to find she couldn't deny it.

'Maybe that was your penance for never having let your mother see your success.'

'And maybe you're making assumptions based on what you think my relationship with her was like.' She bristled unexpectedly. 'Maybe my relationship with my mother was never particularly good, especially considering how she venerated my sorry excuse for a father her entire married life.'

Her words seemed to charge the air. She could almost see it crackling before her eyes.

'I presume you had a stellar relationship with your mother before she died,' she snapped before she could stop herself.

'Not really. I never knew my father. He ditched us before I was even born. But, like your mother, mine exalted him my entire life.' His expression was so impassive that it was impossible to tell what he was really thinking. And yet she desperately wanted to know.

'She'd been a chambermaid before I came along,' he continued. 'Possibly her favourite recrimination to me, from my earliest memory through to her death, was that he would have lifted her from that life...if only I had never come along.'

'Sorry—' she pulled a face, appalled at her own self-centred outburst '—I shouldn't have lost my temper.'

'Is that your idea of a temper?' he challenged, his voice still giving nothing away, although now he had one trademark eyebrow cocked. 'It's remarkably...restrained.'

'Don't worry,' she announced before she caught herself, desperate to lift the mood from whatever trench she'd just been digging. 'I'm sure you're unrestrained enough for the both of us.'

Where the heck had that come from?

The air around them shifted, closing in on her like summer skies before a thrilling storm.

'Careful, Octavia, that could be taken as something approaching an invitation.'

A wiser woman might have paid heed to the note in his voice. The warning sign that she should start treading carefully.

The problem was that she'd spent her whole life being careful. She couldn't put her finger on what it was about Lukas that was so different, but suddenly she didn't want to be that overly retiring version of herself any more.

'I do hope so.' She held his gaze. 'It's *Oti*. Calling me by my full name won't alleviate whatever this…this thing is between us.'

'That's enough… *Oti*.'

It seemed she'd scored a direct hit when she hadn't really even known what she was doing. Lukas's jaw clenched so tightly that she could see the muscle twitching.

'I did tell you, back on our wedding day, that you risked being all mouth and no trousers.'

Did she really just tease him on a sexual level? Her? Who had less experience than anyone she knew?

'I said *that's enough*.'

She wasn't even sure that he'd opened his mouth to speak. The words seemed to hiss out of him, the most deliciously dangerous warning.

'What a shame, Lukas…'

'If you can't silence yourself—' his voice

throbbed in the space that separated them '—then trust me, Octavia, I will do it for you.'

He moved out of his seat so fast that she didn't have time to process what was happening. But, unaccountably, she found herself hauled to her unsteady feet and pressed up against his solid, hewn chest, her head as light-headed as if she were drunk.

Maybe she was. But not on the wine.

'I warned you,' he growled. And she recognised that tautness in his voice, as though he fought to rein himself in.

Suddenly, that was the last thing she wanted.

'You did warn me,' she agreed all too huskily. 'But I never was very good at following instructions.'

Then, before he could set her aside, just as he had done a few nights earlier, she surged against him and pressed her lips to his.

CHAPTER EIGHT

HE HADN'T INTENDED to kiss her.

He'd intended merely to…intimidate her. To stop her from talking. From telling him how he'd felt about her all those months ago. And how he'd come to choose her as his future bride.

He had sworn to himself, those few nights ago, that he would never touch her again after his alarming lack of control.

In fact, Lukas had rapidly come to the conclusion that staying away from this particular woman would be in both of their interests.

But still it took all his resolve to break the kiss and set her aside. More gently this time than he had the other night.

'You don't have to do this, Oti,' he rasped out, ignoring the fact that his body was clamouring for her. 'The money is yours. No strings.'

'And if I want to?' she managed breathlessly. Almost making him surrender right there, on the spot.

He growled, forcing himself to cross the room. To put that space he'd thought about between them.

'You don't want to.'

And then he left the living room and stalked down the hallway to his suite. Stepping through the doors, he stared at his empty bedroom and wondered what the hell was going on that he still lusted after this woman with such intensity.

He didn't hear the click of the door. He didn't even realise she had stepped through the connecting archway between their bedrooms until she said his name, and he turned around.

And his body went into overdrive.

His sweet bride, his shy Oti, was standing against the door wearing nothing but a lace lingerie set—in cherry-red this time—and a pair of *Do me* heels. And it was killing him not to simply obey.

'Go back in your room,' he managed hoarsely.

'I don't think so.' She laughed softly, and he wondered if she knew he heard the nervousness.

'Octavia. I'm not going to tell you again.'

She took another step forward. 'Thank goodness for that. Too much rejection could damage a woman's ego.'

He wasn't a green, inexperienced adolescent. He knew women—and their bodies—as well as he knew his own.

Better, perhaps.

He could read the short, shallow breaths which indicated her interest as easily as he could read the hard, pert nipples that virtually called out for him to touch. His eyes had alighted on those sleek, endless legs of hers. He hadn't been able to stop imagining them wrapped around his waist—or, better yet, draped over his shoulders—since the other night.

The memory of those scraps of electric blue lace that barely concealed her modesty still haunted his dreams. Waking and sleeping.

But he could also read the uncertainty in her eyes.

'This isn't what you want. I can read it in your expression.'

And still she advanced into his room, his space, and he knew what was coming. He thought he was ready. Prepared. His hands prepared to snag her wrists, to hold her away, to *control* this spiralling situation.

'This is *exactly* what I want, Lukas. I'm just terrified you'll throw me out again.'

And he intended to resist her. He really did. But then she took a final step and he caught her scent—soft, fresh, vaguely floral, and that gentle musk that was all woman—and every thought tumbled from his head.

Need punched through him. So hard that he didn't know how he had stayed standing. He had never, *not once*, wanted a woman the way he'd wanted Oti. Still wanted her now. With an uncharacteristic recklessness. As if he'd never had anyone else before.

Dazed, all Lukas could see was images of Oti, stretching in front and behind him. And then she put that hot, sharp mouth of hers on his and something detonated inside him, blowing up any sane thought in the process.

Before he knew it, his hand curled around that elegant neck of hers and he hauled her all-too-willing body to his, revelling in the way she melded herself to him as if it was the most natural thing in the world.

He wanted to lift her into his arms, carry her across to his bed and spread her out on it. And then he wanted to feast on her as if she were his own private buffet.

Lukas had no idea how he managed not to do any of these things. Instead, he took his time. He let her mouth explore his in her own time, as if she was still in control the way she thought she was.

Then again, maybe she was. Or maybe neither of them were?

So he indulged himself. Kissing her over and over, deeper, harder, revelling in the slide of her tongue over his, triumphing in those greedy little sounds she made at the back of her throat.

And the only thought in his head was that he didn't want it to end.

More.

The word pounded through him with every thump of his heart. Like a drumbeat that thundered in his veins.

Every taste of her was like a drug, slipping through him and leaving him feeling more intoxicated than he thought he'd ever felt in all his years.

Slowly, almost lazily, Lukas allowed his free hand to travel her body. Starting with the long, sensuous line of her spine which he made his fingers walk down with excruciating deliberation, relishing the shivers which his teasing elicited from her.

She arched into him, pressing her breasts against him, abrading her nipples against his chest as though she couldn't stand not to be touched any longer. And he found he rather liked that image.

Lukas tore his mouth from hers, allowing his fingers, his mouth, his tongue to begin their wondrous journey of discovery. To trace their way down her jaw, down that sensitive column of her throat and to the hollow at the base.

He thought the needy groans she made might actually kill him. As if a storm was raging through him. Only the voice of reason telling him why this was a bad idea holding him back.

But he couldn't bring himself to care. Not with his bride pressing her body to his as though she couldn't get close enough, the carnal sounds she made racing along his sex as surely as if it were her very tongue.

And he stopped pretending he had any control left whatsoever where his new bride was concerned.

Oti was sure that he was going to drive her insane with need. Somewhere along the line, she seemed to have lost the control she'd thought she had. She wasn't sure that she cared.

Not when her aching, heavy breasts were pressed so deliciously into Lukas's rock of a chest, and every movement he made chafed them like some kind of exquisite torture. And somehow she couldn't remember why she'd ever thought it was a bad idea to consummate this marriage of theirs.

Or that she'd been trying to seduce him for any other reason but this driving, primal need that she had never even known that she possessed.

He seemed intent on glutting himself on every inch of her, learning her curves with his hands, then his mouth. He dropped down her body, worshipping every last swell and dip, cupping her backside in his hands as his mouth brushed over her stomach, and abdomen, and...*dear Lord...* lower.

And then she was being swept up, carried across the room and laid out on his bed whilst Lukas shouldered her legs apart, the darkest, hungriest, wildest expression in that grey stare of his. It made a fluttering chase through her whole body.

'I don't… I haven't…'

'I have,' he muttered darkly.

Then, his eyes not leaving hers for a moment as she watched, transfixed, he lowered his head and licked his way inside her.

Oti combusted. Like a thousand glorious sparks firing off all at once. Like the most spectacular fireworks. It was nothing she'd ever known before. How could it have been?

As Lukas used his mouth, his tongue, to trace her core and dip into her silken heat, all she could do was surrender to him. Moaning with each taunting stroke and bucking against him when she couldn't help herself any longer. And when he laughed, a low, deep sound that vibrated against her very sex, she thought she would shatter into a million tiny shards.

He teased her and toyed with her. Knowing exactly what she needed to carry her out on wave after wave of incredible sensation, whilst he built the storm inside her. Higher and higher. Her hips rocked and jolted, chained to the rhythm that he was setting. Performing the dance that he wanted her to perform.

She didn't care. Just so long as he never, *never* stopped.

And then she felt that final wave swelling beneath her. Lifting higher than she'd ever been before. Panic—banished until that moment—rushed back into her, racing through her body and threatening to overwhelm her.

'Lukas...' She barely recognised her own voice, as breathless and urgent as it sounded.

But, as though he knew exactly what she was feeling, he grazed one hand over her body, making her belly tremble as it skimmed the skin. Then, suddenly, he slid a finger inside her and did something magical with his mouth, and Oti was hurled straight back into the glory of those rolling waves.

This time was all the more devastating than before. With every sweep of his tongue she shook and she shook, spinning higher and higher and more out of control. And then Lukas did something magical, and those last flimsy threads holding Oti to reality were broken.

She was gone. Spiralling up into nothingness with a cry so primal that it surely couldn't have been her. It was as if she were fragmenting. Splintering into so many pieces that she doubted they could ever be put back together properly again. She doubted *she* could ever be put back together again.

She had no idea how long she soared, but when

she finally, *finally* came back to herself, it was to find Lukas moving up the bed and gathering her in his arms as though she was something infinitely precious.

But that was fanciful. And foolish. Sex was sex, and...love was love. Only a fool would confuse the two.

So then you're a fool.

But she didn't have time to dwell. As he rolled onto his back, he carried her with him, settling her down on top of him, his solid, velvety length pressing against her wet heat. And she shivered again, though this time for a slightly different reason.

'Lukas...'

'Stunning,' he breathed, his hand reaching up to cup her breasts and making her bite her lip again.

Was it the incredible sensations or the intensity of his gaze that emptied her head of all rational thought? She didn't know; she could only hear her own breathing, shallow and panting slightly, as he reached between them and traced her swollen core again.

Then, suddenly, he was lined up and Oti found herself waiting, *needing*, desire overcoming anything else she might—or perhaps ought—to be feeling.

And finally, as his eyes locked with hers and she forgot how to breathe, she moved her hands to cover his as they cupped her hips and let him plunge inside her.

It hurts.

Oti stiffened as her fists shot out involuntarily and slammed hard against his unforgiving chest. The pain lanced though her, searingly hot and so very, very sharp that it chased every bit of air from her lungs so that she couldn't even breathe.

He was much too big, much too thick, much too *everything*...so deep inside her. Though, slowly, it dawned on her that he was no longer moving. That he too had gone still, holding her above him with an impressive self-control of which—she was vaguely aware—any other man would have been incapable.

She couldn't move, couldn't speak, couldn't even bring herself to meet Lukas's gaze, though there was no way to avert her face so that he couldn't look at her. Not that she needed to. She could tell by the way her skin burned that he was glowering at her.

That he was furious.

'Are you going to explain this?' he bit out at last, a dangerous edge to his tone despite the quiet, too-controlled pitch that he employed.

A sudden sob made its way up through her and it was all she could do to swallow it back. How had she been so foolish as to think she could deceive Lukas? That he wouldn't discover she was some untried, untested virgin?

His opinion of her had already been low. It seemed that she couldn't even seduce a man without showing her abject lack of experience. And now he wanted her to *explain* herself.

Oti shook her head, helpless against the sting of bitter tears as they welled behind her eyes.

'Ahh, don't cry, Oti.' His tone changed in an instant. It softened in a way she hadn't heard him speak before. 'Not because of a man like me. I'm no good. I'm not worth it.'

Oti's eyes flew to his before she realised what she was doing.

He sounded so…*different*, and she couldn't put her finger on what that emotion was which skittered across his impossibly handsome face, but she knew it was better than what had gone before. And he was still *there*, inside her. Filling her. Stretching her.

What was she to think?

'You should have told me, though,' he added with a slight frown.

'And you would have believed me, of course.'

She didn't know how she kept her tone light. Conversational. Not that it seemed to lessen the impact on Lukas. Another dark cloud crossed his features and Oti waited for him to deny it, but he didn't even attempt to do so. She wasn't sure if that made it better or worse.

'I don't blame you.' The words tumbled out before she'd realised she was going to speak. 'I played my part as the party girl at one time. Not to mention, my father put enough rumours out there about my lifestyle, my partying.'

'I should have asked.'

'Like I said, you wouldn't have listened, and I can understand why.'

'I'm listening now.'

'Now?' She snapped her head to him, praying he couldn't read all the embarrassment that was surely written all over her face. 'With you... *inside* me?'

'I can think of a better time,' he drawled. 'But that boat sailed when you walked into my bedroom looking like a damned siren.'

She shouldn't let his words heat her so easily. And still she felt the grin tug at her mouth.

'A siren?'

'A damned irresistible one,' he groaned. 'And now I find out you were saving yourself.'

'I wasn't saving myself...' She paused, acutely aware that he was still so deep inside her. It seemed like such an odd time to be holding such a conversation. 'I just...didn't find anyone I liked enough.'

Lukas groaned again. Emphatically.

'That's hardly the best thing to tell a guy who's just become your first. It tends to inflate the ego.'

'Really?' she murmured. 'Well, if it helps, I can tell you that you've been a disappointment.'

'A disappointment?' he growled, clearly taken aback.

'A terrible, terrible disappointment,' she teased. Because somehow, in spite of all her lack of experience, he'd made her feel powerful. And utterly desirable. 'It's supposed to be about shattering my earth and rocking my world, is it not? And yet I feel quite…unmoved.'

'Is that so?' Lukas remarked drily.

'It is.' She fought to keep a straight face. 'Because if…'

Lukas began to shift. Slowly drawing out of her, then back in, not so deep this time. Oti caught her breath and waited for the pain, but this time, though it felt odd, the searing sensation had gone, replaced instead by a dull ache. Then, gradually, as he began to move in a lazy rhythm inside her, that ache too began to dissipate.

Little by little, she began to move her hips to meet his, following an instinct that she didn't recognise. Testing him and learning him, even as he moved himself so carefully above her.

Her hands had long since released from their fists, and now she pressed her palms against the solid wall of Lukas's chest, allowing herself to feel the definitive beat of his heart and letting his heat seep into her. Revelling in the way that same heat spread through her, warming her. As if he could heal her…if only she might let him.

And, fanciful or not, Oti finally surrendered, giving in to everything as she'd told herself she must never do.

She forgot about the circumstances of their marriage and she simply relaxed into the moment. Into the incredibly glorious slide of their bodies, so intertwined that she couldn't have said where she ended and he began.

As though she were handcrafted to fit him.

There was nothing but her and Lukas, and that incredible fire he was building within her. Stoking it slowly but surely with every roll of his hips and every pull out and thrust in. Making everything in her world hotter and brighter with each passing moment. Its intensity terrified her and thrilled her in equal measure.

It felt like a lifetime before she came back to herself, floating on sensations she had never experienced before, she'd never even dreamed about, just as nerve endings she hadn't known existed still fired for an age afterwards.

But when she did come back to herself, it was to see Lukas walking back into the bedroom, still gloriously naked, which at least gave her confidence that he wasn't making a bolt for it.

'So—' she licked her lips as she tentatively sat up '—where do we go from here?'

'From here?' he said slowly. Scooping her into his arms, he carried her through to where a hot bath was running, before lowering her in and then sliding in behind her. 'You start to talk to me.'

'What is it I should tell you?' Oti asked a few minutes later. After he'd taken a sponge and squeezed it over her exquisite body.

He was still trying to get his head around the discovery that she'd been a virgin. Still trying to work out how a woman so intelligent and beautiful could possibly have still been untouched.

'Shall we start with the obvious?' he muttered gently, unable to help himself from lifting a wet curl from her neck and dropping a kiss where it had lain.

His body was already—impossibly—beginning to tighten again with need. As though he hadn't just had her—his *wife*—less than ten minutes earlier.

'You want to know why I was still a virgin,' she said flatly.

'For a start.' He dropped another kiss, and her body relaxed just a fraction.

They didn't speak for a moment, the sound of gently splashing water filling the room instead. But then Oti drew in a breath, as though steadying herself, and she began.

'I told you that I picked myself up when I was nineteen, right after my mum died.'

He didn't answer. He didn't need to. He just kept slowly sponging her down.

'But I didn't tell you why I went off the rails in the first place.'

'Take your time,' he murmured when she paused again, this time clearly waiting for some kind of response.

She gave an almost imperceptible dip of her head.

'When I was fifteen I was attacked.'

'Attacked how? Sexually?' Lukas bit out, stilling for a moment, unprepared for the anger that stabbed through him at her unexpected admission. She stiffened again, and he instinctively resumed his ministrations.

'Sort of.' She sucked in a deep breath. 'It was on some holiday, on a beach one night. My family…and the Rockman family.'

Lukas didn't know how he controlled himself. How he didn't spit out the next question.

'One of the Earl's sons?'

'Yes,' she admitted almost soundlessly.

Whatever he'd felt before about the way the Earl—his biological father, for want of any other term—had treated his mother, it was nothing compared to the sheer violence he felt at the knowledge that one of his sons had attacked Oti.

'He raped you?' Lukas rasped out.

'He tried to.' She hunched her shoulders and Lukas had to clench the sides of the bath not to drag her around. Just to give her space.

'I was lucky… Edward came looking for me

and he found us in time…before anything serious happened.'

'You were…okay?' Lukas demanded, immediately regretting his choice of words.

Of course she hadn't been *okay*.

'Edward went mad. I think he would have killed him if I hadn't pulled him away. But when he told our parents, and they told us not to upset the Rockmans by making a big deal of it, he really went crazy.'

'Your parents said what?'

Lukas didn't know how he stayed calm. It was only because he knew that him blowing up would be the last thing that Oti needed.

'That's when our family really started to come apart. I went crazy, turning into that girl we all know so well from the press. I drank, tried drugs and generally wasted my life. But the one thing I couldn't stand to do was be around boys, or men. And I haven't had a serious relationship since.

'Meanwhile, Edward couldn't stand to be around any of us. I think he blamed himself for not being there sooner to stop it getting even as far as it did.'

'I can understand that.' Lukas barely recognised his own voice. 'I can't believe that you could stand to be near your parents after that.'

'I couldn't.' She shook her head, but he noticed her shoulders were relaxing slightly and she was beginning to sit up straight again. 'I think it's why I turned so wild.'

'But you picked yourself up. You got to medical school. That's to be commended.'

'Only once my mother had died and I felt like living that lifestyle was only punishing myself. I was lucky that I'd got good grades through school, despite all my coasting. But once I got my head down I worked hard, and I became a doctor.'

And then her brother's accident had happened, and she'd ended up running away to Africa.

Lukas shook his head, his mind still grappling with everything that he'd discovered in the past twenty-four hours. 'I can only imagine what you've been going through these past years.'

He needed to stay focused and strong, for Oti. The wife he hadn't wanted, but now found he couldn't remember life without. The woman who hadn't even felt able to tell him that she had been a virgin.

He felt like a complete cad.

If he was any kind of decent man he would walk away now. They'd agreed from the start that there would be no physical side to their marriage, and he should have stuck to that. He should never have given in to his overwhelming desire for her; he should have been strong enough for both of them.

He owed her that much.

And then she spun around abruptly in the bath, and he definitely wasn't expecting the bright, almost dazzling expression on her face.

'I haven't been going through anything, Lukas,' she told him earnestly. 'Not any more. I've been focused on the positives and I've been living my best life being the doctor I always wanted to be in South Sudan.'

Lukas was still fighting to make sense of everything she was telling him. Revelation after revelation had fallen from her lips, building up a picture of a woman who was a million miles away from the creature he'd told himself, a matter of months ago, that she was.

She made him feel all at sea. And humbled.

'I'm so sorry.' He shook his head. 'If it hadn't been for this marriage you would still be out in Africa, doing the job you love so much. And this...*us* should never have happened. Go back— I won't stop you.'

He began to lift himself out of the bath, to give Oti her space, vowing to himself that he would never touch her again, when she grabbed his wrists and held him in place.

'Lukas—' she cut him off, not even trying to conceal the excitement in her tone '—you could come out with me. Even just for a month or two. See what I do... *Did*.'

'Oti...'

'You asked me if there was anything you could

do,' she challenged. 'This is it. Come back to South Sudan with me.'

'Oti…'

But it appeared that now she had the proverbial bit between her teeth she wasn't about to let go.

'Please, Lukas. We'll call it our honeymoon.'

And it should concern him more that his head told him to let her go whilst his…chest pulled tight with the effort of stopping himself from agreeing.

CHAPTER NINE

LESS THAN A week later, after an eleven-hour flight from London to Juba, the capital, and then a fifty-minute flight to a small airstrip in the middle of nowhere—the closest serviceable one given the season—Lukas found himself with Oti in South Sudan.

The paperwork for him to join her had taken a bit more work, as he'd not been on the charity's books nor been through their lengthy application process. But it never failed to strike Lukas just how far limitless pockets of cash could get a person. Coupled with the fact that they'd clearly been prepared to move heaven and earth to get Oti back there.

It was crazy how the more he was around her the more he wanted her. Like an addiction, when the only addiction he'd ever had before had been to succeed and drag himself out of the council estate where he'd spent the formative years of his life.

They were four hours into their five-hour drive

to the medical camp when they passed a woman on the road carrying a screaming, rigid baby, its arms locked in an uncomfortable outstretched position.

Lukas wasn't surprised when the driver stopped the car and Oti leapt out. He followed out of instinct, but it was odd, after a professional lifetime of being the person people automatically looked to in order to resolve any number of problems, to now be the person relegated to standing on the sidelines watching.

The only plus side was that it afforded him the opportunity to watch Oti in what was clearly her environment. She had a quiet authority about her that was eminently watchable. A grace and an efficiency, just like she'd demonstrated that day back home when she'd helped the woman deliver her baby at the roadside.

Oti clearly cared deeply about her patients, just as there was no doubt in Lukas's mind that she loved her job. And marriage to him had nearly robbed her of all of that, yet she'd been prepared to do so out of love for her brother.

She made him feel humbled. Which was why there was no way that he was going to spoil things for Oti by letting her see his discomfort at quite how redundant he already felt out here. All he could do was be here in case she needed him for now, and once he got to camp she'd assured him there would be plenty of non-medical jobs to occupy any volunteer.

He fervently hoped that was true. He hadn't had a full week away from work since he'd written his first app at fifteen; there was no way he could sit and twiddle his thumbs for the next couple of months.

Keeping his distance by the four-by-four, Lukas watched as Oti chatted to the mother, mostly using her own grasp of the language, with their driver and translator standing by for backup, though she didn't appear to need it.

It wasn't long before Oti headed back over to him, and he wasn't surprised that the relieved mother was in tow.

'This is Larhan and her baby. I suspect he's contracted neonatal tetanus, so the earlier we start treatment, the more chance he has of survival.'

'She was walking to the camp?' He didn't know why he felt so shocked. 'It's an hour's drive away. And even at our slow driving speed on these so-called roads, there is no way someone walking would get there before nightfall.'

'That's why we're taking her with us,' Oti confirmed. 'I'll sit in the back with them, but her baby is going to need space. Could you get the rucksacks out and keep them in the front with you? It'll be tight, but rather that than them falling against him. He's in enough pain as it is.'

'Are the limbs meant to be locked out like that?' He frowned. 'I mean, obviously they're not *meant* to be but...'

'I know what you mean.' She even offered him a smile. 'The muscle rigidity is caused by the toxin acting on the baby's central nervous system.'

'But he's...what...a few weeks old?' He had no idea about babies, but he looked small. 'How did he get tetanus?'

'Given that he's only five days old, I'd say it's likely he contracted it due to poor umbilical-cord-cutting practices when he was born. A dirty blade or, more often out here, the practice of drying out the cord by sealing it with cow dung. Sort of like a poultice. We see it a lot out here.'

'Isn't the cow sacred to some of the tribes out here?' he reflected carefully.

'Exactly, but right now this baby is suffering with spasms, and if we don't get him back quickly then he'll most likely die. In our camp, around three in every four babies that we see die of it, usually because they don't get to us in time, but also because we have limited resources out here.'

Shock ran through Lukas as he hauled the rucksacks onto his back and ran them around to the front of the vehicle. He wasn't sure what he'd expected when he'd agreed to travel out here with her, but it hadn't been this. It was quite a rude awakening.

'It gets worse, though,' Oti added quietly as she came around with the last bag. 'We call it the silent killer because we only get to see about five per cent of the babies who suffer from it. As far as we can estimate, many thousands more die at home, in terrible pain.'

'But even if we get him back to your camp in time, the probability is that he won't survive?'

She didn't answer. She didn't need to. Instead, he followed her around the back of the four-by-four to help her and the mother and baby into the back. Then he slammed the old creaking door as gently as he could and prepared to push the vehicle out of the boggy mud where it had sunk after being stationary for even that short period.

At least that way he felt useful.

And an hour later they were finally at the compound, a high brush fence surrounding baked clay brick huts and various tents, from nine-by-nines to larger marquee-style offerings.

He watched Oti leap down into a handful of other medical volunteers who looked to be coming out to greet them.

Their expressions of delight and welcome switched instantly to professional mode as Oti approached, their gaze dropping from her to the wailing baby in her arms.

'This is Shangok. He's five days old. We saw

his mother, Larhan, about an hour down the road to the camp, so we brought them in. As far as I can gather, he was born a healthy two point eight kilograms, and for the first few days he fed, slept and cried as normal. Yesterday, however, he stopped feeding and began to turn stiff. He hasn't slept or stopped crying since.'

'MNT?' one of her colleagues posited.

Oti gave a curt bob of her head. 'I suspect so.'

'We'll take him inside and get treatment started if you want to get settled in?'

'No.' Oti shook her head. 'I'll do it. Give me one moment.'

'You're jumping straight back into work,' Lukas said as she hurried over to him.

She looked momentarily abashed. 'Do you mind?'

'Would it matter if I did?' He smiled despite himself. 'This is why we're here, is it not? You want to show me the role you love.'

The brilliance of her smile punched through him. In all the time he'd known her—and, admittedly, it wasn't that much—he'd never seen her smile like that. As if she was truly happy being back, despite the circumstances of their arrival. Her joy was truly intoxicating.

'I'm sorry.' She was already heading away from him. 'They'll want to get him into a quiet environment with little stimuli, so if I don't go now then I won't be able to go in afterwards.'

'Go.' He waved her away with his hand, even though he didn't have a clue what he was supposed to do next.

'Look for the big boss. She'll tell you where your *tukul* is, and then we'll compare house guests when we meet next. Mine has a hedgehog who likes to snuffle about in the middle of the night.'

Before he could answer, she had turned around and hurried off.

Everyone seemed to have a task, a purpose, hurrying around quickly. The sooner he was one of them the better.

It was a good couple of hours before Oti finally left the medical tent, making her way across the compound to the *tukul* where she'd been told Lukas was, still shocked that no one appeared to have recognised him yet. It felt like fate that he hadn't shaved since their wedding, because it was amazing what a couple of weeks' worth of facial hair and a baseball cap could do.

To her, it was still obvious that Lukas Woods was the man beneath, but to people who weren't expecting him to be out here in the first place it was enough to cast shadows over the sharper contours of his face, to soften his telltale square jaw and to conceal the giveaway cleft in his chin.

She doubted they would get away with it for too long, but she would be grateful for every day they were able to settle in without too much scrutiny. Hopefully enough time to help them find a groove.

She could still hardly believe that he had agreed to come out here with her. As though he actually cared about her, as though she mattered to him. And it didn't matter how much she told herself it was all deeply fanciful and ridiculous— every time Lukas watched her with those intense granite-grey eyes she felt as though he was seeing her for the first time all over again.

But right now she should check he was settling in before heading back to her own old hut for a bit of alone time. She could hardly wait.

Sure about that? a voice questioned silently in her head. Oti ignored it.

'Knock-knock,' she began as she reached the open door to one of the larger *tukuls*.

A grin pulled at her lips despite everything. No doubt he'd already realised how sweltering it was in those huts, until the temperature dropped later in the night.

'Are you settling in okay?'

The hut was usually reserved for the main project managers or surgeons. It was about twice the size of her *tukul*, complete with a king-size bed and a new-looking mosquito net. She was used to an old one that had been repaired at least a couple of times, using silver tape. Why wasn't she surprised the billionaire was being treated like royalty?

'I've been…*playing house*, it seems,' he replied drily, his head turning to look at her. 'Unpacking as best I can, given that all clothes have to be bagged to keep any unpleasant insects or arachnids from crawling into them.'

'It's a bit of an art form,' she agreed, laughing. Then she spotted her own half-empty rucksack. 'Wait, why did you unpack my stuff? I have my own *tukul*—it's just over there.'

Turning to point between a few other huts, she noticed a decoration on the door that she hadn't left there. As though someone else was now occupying it.

'You *had* your own *tukul*,' Lukas corrected quietly.

Something flip-flopped inside her.

'Well, it doesn't matter.' She forced a smile. 'I'm sure my new one will be fine. Not as salubrious as yours, of course.'

'This is our *tukul*, Oti.'

She blinked at him, a cold sensation rushing over her body as she stood statuelike, followed by a rush of heat which she preferred not to dwell on.

'It can't be. It's too…' she bit back the word *intimate* '…big. And it's usually reserved for people more senior than me.'

'Your project chief said it was going spare and she thought, as a newly married couple, we would appreciate it. I wasn't about to lay out the details of our arrangement to her.'

'No, obviously not.' She bit her lower lip.

'I suspect you'll have a fair few questions to answer next time you see people, though. She was rather shocked you'd never mentioned me before.'

She could well imagine it. Everyone had been so focused on the baby, Shangok, that there hadn't been chance for anyone to ask her about her sudden change in marital status. But tonight, and tomorrow, Oti had no doubt there would be a veritable barrage of questions fired her way.

'But we can't share a hut, Lukas.' Her voice shook and there wasn't a darn thing she could do about it. Her eyes slid, almost against her will, to the king-size bed. 'We can't share...*that*.'

They hadn't been intimate again since that one night, almost a week ago. Not that she hadn't enjoyed it—*more* than enjoyed it—but after that bath, and her shocking revelation, Lukas had closed and bolted the door between their suites and practically moved out of their—*his*—home and into his city centre office, making it clear that he had no intention of a repeat performance.

She'd tried not to let it hurt her. Clearly he was the kind of man who liked the thrill of the chase more than he liked a sure thing—but hadn't she known that about him already?

And he hadn't been the one to instigate that night, had he?

Either that, or she'd been so appallingly bad in bed that he didn't want a repeat performance. Just because she'd found their night together so wholly electrifying didn't mean that Lukas had been equally enthused.

Oti felt a hot flush spread over her cheeks; how had she failed to recognise that at the time?

'I agree—it isn't ideal.'

'Ideal?' She tried for another laugh, but it sounded flat.

From the safety of the doorway, she once again eyed up the king-size mattress on the old pallet frame. There was also a battered old dresser desk, a rickety chair and a newly woven rug.

As *tukuls* went, it looked lovely. And that wouldn't do at all.

She and Lukas might have pretended to the objecting board members of his various companies that they were going on a delayed honeymoon, but that didn't actually mean it had to feel like one.

'We should have a hut each,' she muttered faintly, not daring to look at Lukas. 'I didn't plan this. You have to understand that.'

'Obviously you didn't plan it.' He had crossed the tiny space before she had a chance to move, his hands going to her shoulders. 'You don't believe that *I* manipulated this situation?'

'Of course not.' Her gaze seemed to be locked with his, and she couldn't have disconnected even if she'd wanted to. 'You made it abundantly clear, even back at the house, that you wouldn't be… inviting any further intimacy between us.'

'Right.' He nodded with evident relief, and she tried not to feel irrationally hurt. 'I'm glad that was clear.'

'But you didn't insist on separate accommodation?' She swallowed heavily.

Even though she tried, there was no suppressing the glimmer of hope that he just might admit it was because a part of him had wanted to share. And then he moved closer to her, so fast that she didn't have time to think. But her heart had time to beat faster.

'This isn't a conversation for other ears,' Lukas muttered tersely, his large hand circling her wrist gently as he tugged her inside.

'No.' He didn't hesitate once the door was closed. 'But only because I believe it would only raise suspicion. After all, we're supposed to be a newly married couple.'

Yanking herself out of his grasp, Oti tried to push back the sense of disappointment that raced through her. It was shamefully telling that she didn't open the door or try to leave. They were alone and, despite everything, her entire body was prickling with awareness.

She swallowed heavily. 'Yet we can't stay here and…share a bed.'

'There's no choice.' His voice held a sort of grimness that made her feel perversely insulted. She wondered what was wrong with her. 'We're married. We're sharing. It's done.'

Oti stared at the bed, then at the floor. She felt like some gauche teenager again, and hated herself for it.

'We're grown adults, not unschooled adolescents,' he pressed on, as if reading her thoughts. She hated the way he could do that. 'I'm sure we can sleep in the same bed without touching each other.'

A memory of their night together slid, unbidden, into her head. He had reached for her so many times that night, as though he could glut on her for ever and still never have enough. He'd made her feel so cherished, so incredible, and she'd never, *ever*, felt like that before.

She'd never thought she was capable of it, especially after the attack.

It was as if Lukas had made her come alive, and she'd suddenly realised what she'd been missing out on all those years. Yet now he was like a different man, keeping her at arm's length and making it clear he didn't remotely feel that same draw, that same desire, whilst she couldn't imagine ever wanting to be with anyone else.

He'd ruined her. And the worst of it was that

if she could go back in time and choose to have one night with Lukas or a lifetime with anyone else, then she wouldn't hesitate to choose him. Every time.

'Of course we can,' she replied, wondering if her voice sounded as hollow to Lukas's ears as it did to hers. She hoped not.

'Besides, you'll be in that hospital eighteen hours a day, from what you've told me, grabbing a few hours' sleep when you can, sometimes working through the night. And I've already been given a list of tasks, so I have plenty to do. We won't even be in here at the same time for much of it.'

'And when we are, we'll be so tired that we'll be asleep before our heads even hit the pillow,' she added, wishing that she could believe that for even a minute.

She couldn't actually imagine anyone being able to sleep if they were sharing a bed with Lukas. She doubted anyone ever had.

Her body signalled its approval instantly.

'Are you okay?' He eyed her closely. 'You appear to be a little flushed.'

'It's a little hot in here, don't you think?' Beginning to babble, she headed for the door. 'Sometimes you marinate in your own sweat in these places. I've known people to pull their beds outside and sleep in the cool air.'

'That's an option,' he replied evenly. 'But

for now, acting like we can actually stand to be around each other would be a start.'

She nodded stiffly, her mind searching for a topic but coming up short. He made it sound so easy. Then again, it probably was easy for him.

In the end, it was Lukas who spoke first. 'How is the baby, anyway?'

'Shangok?'

Did his voice sound hoarser than usual? No, it was no doubt just her imagination. At least this was a topic she could discuss with some ease.

'Shangok. Yes.'

She lifted her shoulders sadly. 'We won't know for a while. That is to say, we're more likely to know if he's getting worse than if he is responding. We put him on a drip, and we'll use as much of our limited resources as we can.'

'Is he still in pain?'

'Incredible pain.' She nodded. 'We inserted an IV line and administered medications to control the muscle spasms, otherwise he'd be unable to move his rigid body yet feel every single one of them.'

'It sounds horrendous.'

'You have no idea.' She sucked in a breath. 'The slightest thing can set a spasm off, from a soft noise to the lightest touch, even a whisper of wind gliding over their skin.'

'I take it that's why you mentioned putting him in an environment with little stimuli?'

'Yes.' No point in thinking about their home—
his home—now. 'The hut we have is darkened,
with a more consistent temperature than elsewhere.'

'And it will be enough?'

He actually sounded as though he cared. But
then, why wouldn't he? He wasn't some heartless
monster. Except, perhaps, where her own traitorous heart was concerned. And that was hardly
his fault, since he'd warned her from the start
that she should know what she was signing up to.

She dragged her mind back to the little baby in
the *tukul*. Would the measures be enough?

'I don't know,' she told him sadly. 'He really
needs human tetanus immune globulin, but our
stores are virtually depleted. There should have
been a supply run a few weeks ago, but the rains
meant that the runways were impassable. Last
time I was here, we had three babies die within
a thirty-hour period.'

'That many? I thought illnesses like tetanus
were virtually eradicated.'

Oti tried to concentrate on the topic at hand
and not the way that his sense of compassion
somehow made him that much *more* than the
man she was already beginning to fall for.

'That doesn't come close to the true extent of
the problem, Lukas. It's estimated that out here,
in the bush, around ninety per cent of births happen in the home, and a high percentage of those

births will result in maternal and neonatal tetanus being contracted when the umbilical cord is cut. Most of the time, they never make it to us—maybe as little as five per cent of the time—and because of the way it moves through the body, the mother and/or the baby will be dead within days.'

'That's…staggering.' His brow pulled up tight, and there was an expression in his gaze which she didn't entirely recognise. 'Surely that can't be across the entire country?'

'It isn't.' She forced a half-smile. 'In the cities, where there are hospitals, the incidence is much lower. The charities and the government have been working together for a long time, establishing vaccine roll-outs and educating people.'

'But out here in the middle of nowhere, not everyone has access to healthcare and so immunisation rates are lower?' he guessed.

'Plus, so many people are displaced.' She nodded, loving the way he took an interest because she did. As though it mattered to him because it mattered to her. 'They have enough trouble finding clean water, food and building new shelter for themselves. And they have their traditional healers—some of whom are actually very good at what they do, and some are completely ineffective. Either way, western-influenced health education is very much a low priority for them.'

'What about vaccine drives? Education drives?'

She was beginning to see what Lukas relished the most. A project. A goal. It gave him purpose.

Just like being out here had always made her feel as if she had value.

She couldn't help wondering if it was tied to the way his mother had worshipped his biological father, despite him abandoning her and Lukas. Just as her self-worth had been damaged the day her parents had refused to side with her over what had happened with the Rockman boy—she didn't even like to think of him by name.

They'd valued money and connections over her well-being. It had taken her years to get over that, and this place had helped.

As had Lukas, though that made no sense.

'Obviously we educate people.' She nodded softly, pushing the confused thoughts from her head. 'Multiple charities, not just HOP, have worked together with the government for years, on huge public awareness and vaccine drives. And we are making ground. But it's an ongoing issue. And money only goes so far, you know. We aren't all billionaires.'

She stopped, horrified, waiting for him to say something.

He didn't speak.

'I wasn't asking for more money,' she choked out, hating how she'd let things get awkward between them.

'I know.'

'I didn't mean…'

'I know.' He silenced her. 'It's been a long few days. I suggest we get some sleep and regroup tomorrow.'

Sleep? How was she supposed to sleep whilst lying in a bed next to Lukas? Not least because all she wanted to do was be close to him, touch him, be touched by him. Just like the other night.

And he didn't want any of that.

'I think sleep is a good idea,' she lied as brightly as she could. 'I'll get changed in the shower block.'

'No, you stay here. I'll change over there. I want to check tomorrow's schedule with one of the guys I met this afternoon, anyway. You may well be asleep by the time I get back.'

'Great.' Another lie. 'Well, see you in the morning, Lukas. Goodnight.'

CHAPTER TEN

DESPITE FEARING THAT she would never be able to sleep with Lukas next to her—his back to hers—Oti woke up the following morning having had one of the most peaceful nights she'd experienced in a while.

The early-morning sounds of camp floated around the *tukul*, but the sound she found her ears straining for was Lukas.

Nothing.

Rolling gingerly onto her back, she turned her head to his side of the bed, only to find that he'd gone. Her stomach lurched, though she told herself not to be so dramatic. Lukas was a notoriously early riser; just because he wasn't here didn't mean he was trying to avoid her.

Stretching out her hand, she checked his side of the bed, to find that it was cold. He'd clearly left some time ago.

To avoid her?

It was a question she couldn't possibly answer, and yet she felt she already knew.

Slipping out of the mosquito nets and throwing on fresh shorts and a T-shirt, Oti slipped into the ablution hut to shower. It was nothing like the glorious, hot power shower that she'd enjoyed back home—back at *Lukas's* home—but it felt familiar and somehow comforting. From the low-pressure, tepid trickle that rolled briefly over her body to dodging the bats above her head, it was everything she'd grown accustomed to over the past four years.

Still, as she dried off and returned to their hut, Oti found herself hoping that he would be back there. But he wasn't.

Eventually, she headed over to check on Shangok, relieved to discover that, whilst there wasn't yet any improvement, he hadn't significantly deteriorated. That, at least, was the best she could hope for at this stage.

By his bedside, the baby's mother could only watch on, her face impassive. And, not for the first time, Oti's chest pulled tight. Death was such a part of life out here, with mothers forced to watch so many sick, dying children that their attitudes were far more stoic than Oti wished they had to be, but that didn't mean they felt the loss any less acutely. Here, the mothers seemed to permanently hold and cradle their babies, which only made tetanus all the more cruel. And it never got easier, trying to explain why—with this particular infection—cradling their suffering babies made it worse, not better.

Offering the mother a small smile and a brief word, Oti made her way from the tetanus hut to the main medical tent and began to familiarise herself with the new cases that had come in during the couple of weeks since she'd left. She was so absorbed in her work that she didn't notice Amelia join her until she felt herself embraced in a huge hug.

'You dark horse.' Her friend laughed. 'You never said anything about getting married. Congratulations!'

Delight swept through Oti, though it was swiftly followed by a stab of guilt.

'I'm sorry I didn't say anything,' she began, returning the embrace. 'I just…'

'I get it—you didn't want to jinx it.'

'Something like that,' Oti lied, feeling another jab of shame, especially when Amelia linked her arm.

'What did they tell me his name is—Luke?'

'Lukas,' Oti clarified, waiting for her friend to connect the dots. But Amelia was already focusing on her patients. 'I'll introduce you later. Maybe at lunch, if there isn't a sudden influx.'

She didn't know why she'd said that. More for something to say than anything else, but her colleague looked up in surprise.

'There's a supply drop coming in at lunchtime.

Your husband went with the loggies to collect it. They left a few hours ago. You didn't know?'

Lukas had already joined the logisticians on a supply run? And notably one that would keep them away from camp for a few days.

Oti plastered a smile on her face. 'Ah, well, I can introduce you when they get back. By the look of all these new cases, we won't be getting out of here for a couple of days, anyway.'

'I hear you.' Amelia offered a wry smile. 'Come on, let me introduce you to Jalka. She was admitted a few days ago after suffering from a miscarriage at fifteen weeks and after carrying out tests we discovered she's suffering from malaria.'

Oti nodded grimly. Out here malaria accounted for just under half the miscarriages and stillbirths that their medical camp saw.

'Haemoglobin levels?'

'Investigative screening showed a level of around half normal levels, at four point eight,' Amelia confirmed. 'We were lucky that her mother was a safe match and prepared to donate blood for her.'

'Great.' It was good to hear that she had a relative.

Superstition often prevented blood donations, and certainly not to a stranger. If the patient didn't have a relative who was a match and cleared by the lab technicians as a safe donor, it was often hard to find any blood to donate.

Consequently, Oti had known the volunteer doctors and nurses come off twenty-hour shifts, only to donate their own blood, in the hope that it might save a life.

'And this was a few days ago?' Oti confirmed.

'Yep, your task today is a relatively pleasant one to get you back into the swing of it.' Her colleague grinned. 'Carry out a final test on Jalka and, hopefully, discharge her with iron tablets. She should be free to return home.'

'Great.' Oti smiled. 'If only they were all that pleasant.'

'À gauche...à gauche,' Lukas relayed to the driver, Jean-Christophe, as he received instructions over the walkie-talkie from the vehicle that had gone ahead of them.

It had been several days of bumpy driving and the recent rains meant it was all only just passable. Even so, they had finally managed to reach the airstrip to collect the supplies and were finally on their way back to camp. To Oti.

He thrust the thought from his mind.

Had it not been for the skill of their drivers, Lukas was fairly certain they'd have been bogged down in mud more than just the once so far.

It had been unexpectedly satisfying leaping out with the rest of the team to push the four-by-four out of the mud and dirt. The physical exertion had somehow helped towards clearing his mind, just as he'd hoped getting out of the compound would do.

Getting away from Oti.

Spending the night next to her in bed, pretending to himself that he didn't ache to simply turn over and haul her back into his arms, had been torturous. If he'd thought it had been challenging those last few days back in the UK, keeping his distance from her by spending most of his time at the office, then being stuck in that compound with her for the next month or so was going to be agonising.

He'd needed to find something to do that would exhaust him both mentally and physically. By the looks of things, working with the logisticians would be an ideal solution. From everything he'd been able to glean so far, there were two main areas of work in the HOP camps. The medical team who took care of all the patients and the logistics team who took care of everything else, from the erection of the tents and huts to the working of the generators, the digging of wells, going on supply runs—the list seemed never-ending.

Just the kind of work that Lukas felt he could really get his teeth into—getting back to the mechanical work he had always enjoyed, even from a kid back in that garage. Before LVW Industries had even been a dream.

And exactly the kind of thing that could help him keep his mind off his new wife.

Right?

'We should have to be stopping soon,' one of the other logisticians in the back, a softly spoken German lad, announced. 'It is time we are stoking the generator in the truck.'

'I'll alert the other vehicles,' Lukas confirmed, picking up the walkie-talkie again, grateful that they had given him something tangible to do rather than just being a useless addition to the team.

They'd claimed it wasn't a big deal, and that they were so shattered that handing over to someone else would free them up to grab a few extra hours' kip in the back seat. But it didn't matter to Lukas so long as he was a valuable member of the team.

He didn't give free rides in business, so he certainly didn't intend to accept them on this posting. And already, he thought, he was beginning to understand why Oti had spent the better part of the past four years so committed to the charity.

'José says there's a bit of a flat area on higher ground a couple of kilometres down the road.' Lukas replaced the handset again. 'He thinks that would be the most logical place to stop. Less chance of any of the vehicles getting bogged down.'

'*D'accord.*' Jean-Christophe signalled his agreement. 'Okay. I stop there. But you are ready for interrogation from José, yes?'

'Sorry?' Lukas turned sharply to the laughing driver.

'You have of the luck, travelling with us. This is first mission in this camp for Alex and me, and we are not knowing Oti much well. But José is knowing her for years. He is nice guy, but he is not knowing about you, and I am thinking that he is not being happy.'

'Something to look forward to, then.' Lukas grinned.

'Yes, indeed.' Jean-Christophe laughed all the harder.

Lukas settled back, unconcerned. He wasn't bothered about José asking him questions, or anyone else for that matter. In truth, the closeness of the team was a good thing. Oti had likened it to a close family and now he could see what she'd meant. And that should make it easier for her when their marriage—their fake marriage—finally came to an end.

She would have this job, and this family, to come back to. A place where she felt safer, surrounded by people who cared about her. So why did the prospect fill him with something that felt less like relief...and more like jealousy?

'There. *Là-bas.*' Lukas indicated suddenly, rounding a bend to see one of the vehicles ahead of them heading up a dirt path on the side of a slight hill.

There had to be a turn-off somewhere; it didn't look as though this road headed that way. It didn't help to peer through the fly-splattered windscreen—water being too much of a luxury to waste too often, especially not on the passenger side—he stuck his head out of the window.

'About one hundred metres—there looks to be a turn-off.'

Really, it was more of a muddy patch, but it looked promising. Jean-Christophe clearly agreed since, as he reached the point Lukas had indicated, he turned the wheel carefully, inching the vehicle between the worst of the mud pit and the rocky outcrop on the other side.

The road—not that it could be called that— was so narrow that Lukas wondered how the truck driver had navigated it without the wheels sliding off the side. But by the time they arrived on the flatter top, the other two vehicles were already parked in a circle along with two more old charity cars he didn't recognise. A small group was gathered around the truck, looking concerned.

Jumping out, Lukas, Jean-Christophe and Alex all hurried over to join them. And as they stepped aside he caught sight of Oti in the middle of the group.

What the hell is she even doing here? he thought as his stomach lurched—but, tellingly, it was a good lurch, not a bad one.

Without a word, they edged slightly away from the group, just as the driver was telling them the generator to the truck had packed in, and Alex the loggie was stepping forward to take a closer look.

'I didn't plan this,' Oti began quietly. 'We just knew you guys were heading back this way, and there's a camp in this direction where we've been intending to run a measles vaccination drive for months. We just didn't have the supplies.'

'So you thought you'd save time and meet us en route.' Lukas kept his tone steady. 'It makes sense.'

What made less sense was quite how erratic his pulse was. He could feel it slamming around, especially at his neck.

'Exactly.' She looked relieved. 'So, we're… good?'

'Sure.'

He didn't feel *good*. He felt something a whole lot more—almost dangerously so. He wanted to say something. Or, worse, *do* something. Like touch her. Taste her.

With deliberate nonchalance, he turned back to the group in time to hear Alex deliver his verdict.

'Looks like the filter, maybe?' he declared. 'But we'd need Clem to fix it.'

'Who's Clem?' Lukas asked as a rumble of concern made its way around the group.

'Clem is mechanic.' Jean-Christophe pulled a face. 'He is being back in camp.'

Another rumble ran around the group. The supplies they'd collected included anti-malaria drugs and tetanus vaccine, along with some other medical supplies which all needed to be kept in a carefully controlled cool environment. Only a working generator could keep the back of the truck cold enough.

'And Clem is only one can fix.' Alex pointed to the generator.

'Unless you can?' Oti ventured hesitantly, looking at him.

'You are mechanic?' Jean-Christophe frowned.

'I used to tinker a bit.'

'He used to build his own racing cars.' Oti stepped in, glancing at him. 'Sorry, but this is no time for false modesty. Edward told me he met you at the racetrack once or twice. And if we don't get this fixed, we could lose a significant amount of the supplies.'

As a murmur of agreement made its way around, Lukas acknowledged her point and peered at the machine. It didn't take him long to determine that Alex was right; it was the fuel filter that needed replacing.

'Do we have any spares?'

'Should have been on supply plane, but no.' Jean-Christophe bunched his shoulders. 'Was expected fifteen days ago. We cannot be keeping much supplies in camp, in case of being attacked of bandits.'

Yeah, Oti had explained to him that everything was kept to a minimum the further out the camps were from any main towns or cities. The more remote, the more they depended on regular supplies. The less they kept on site, the less of a target the hospital, the staff and the patients would be to any potential thieves.

In a roundabout way, Lukas supposed it made sense, though it didn't help in situations like this.

'There's nothing?' he checked. 'Not even an old generator?'

'Yes, old generator in car,' one of the other drivers jumped in suddenly. 'But is not work.'

'It doesn't matter if it works.' Lukas thought quickly. 'It's the fuel filter I need. It just might do.'

'I get, I get.' The driver hurried over to his vehicle as Lukas began working at the generator in the truck.

'Is not same type generator.' The driver frowned, bringing it over. 'Filter does not fit.'

'Let me see?' demanded Lukas, stretching out his hand. He investigated it closely. 'No, it isn't the same, but I reckon I could file the leads down and jimmy something up.'

'Who is this Jimmy?' Jean-Christophe frowned as the group began to crowd around Lukas. 'We backing up, yes? Giving the man space to work. Showing us that he is not being our little Oti's plus one after all.'

'Jean-Christophe...' Oti sounded agitated but a laugh sprung out of Lukas.

'Is that what they're calling me?'

He realised he hadn't heard himself quite that relaxed or happy in a long time. Ironic, given the situation. But it had been creeping up on him for the past month or so.

Ever since his marriage.

'Oti's plus one, *sí*,' confirmed José, clearly delighted he wasn't taking it personally.

'Right, well—' sliding the screwdriver inside and prising the filter out with a grunt, Lukas cast the grimy diesel-covered part a triumphant grin '—we'd better show everyone—including my beautiful new wife—that I'm more than that, don't you think, gentlemen?'

And he told himself that his chest didn't swell when Oti flushed that delicious shade of pink that he was beginning to get to know so well.

Not in the slightest.

'You know you're the hero of the week?'

Lukas glanced up as she approached. His face

was already taking on a golden colour from the sun, making him all the more handsome, if that was even possible.

She valiantly tried to stop her heart from hammering in her chest.

'Is that so?' he drawled.

The hammering increased in intensity.

'Everyone is buzzing about you.' She made herself laugh, looking around the small group as they waved their newly acquired supply run beers in the air and turned up the volume a little more on the music. 'You can't go anywhere without being a success, can you?'

'I just rigged up a bit of filter repair.' He brushed it off in typical Lukas fashion. 'It was a bit hammy, but it did the job. The vehicles are with Clem, the mechanic, now for some proper repairs.'

'Don't underestimate your value,' she told him, suddenly serious. 'If you hadn't cooled that truck in time, we wouldn't have much in the way of usable medicines, and we sorely needed everything we got. The rains here really impacted our supplies this past month.'

'Speaking of which, you rushed off so quickly to do that medical drive, once we got the truck generator working again, that I didn't get chance to ask how the baby is—Shangok, right?'

'He developed sleep apnoea that second day and the spasms increased, so we feared the worst.' She didn't tell him that neither she nor Amelia had gone to bed that night, or the next day. 'Then, just as we feared he was starting to slip away, the drugs must have begun to kick in and everything stopped getting worse. And then, all of a sudden, he began to improve. Just a little, but enough to give us hope.'

'And now, with these drugs?'

She nodded, hopeful but not wanting to be unrealistic.

'Now he really stands a chance of recovery. I hope he does,' she couldn't help but emphasise.

She eyed him carefully before speaking again.

'Did you take the mission with the loggies to keep away from me?'

She noted that he took a long pull of his beer before answering.

'I think staying away from each other, at least in an intimate setting, is for the best, wouldn't you agree?'

'Why?' She shook her head, careful to keep her voice low.

'Because the last thing I should have done was sleep with you that night.'

'Was it really that bad for you?' Oti blurted out suddenly, even as she squeezed her eyes shut and wished she could swallow the words back.

'What?'

'Forget it.' She shook her head violently. She was such an idiot.

'Oti…'

'No, really.' She backed up, hitting a wooden pillar in her haste. 'Forget I said anything.'

'You think it was bad for me?'

Fight or flight?

Back home, she might well have done the latter. But out here she always felt different. Bolder. Stronger. More herself.

Straightening her shoulders, Oti looked directly at him. 'Obviously it was, because you've been very fastidious about not being alone with me ever since that night.'

She could hear her heart beating in the long pause before he answered.

'I was giving you space.'

'Please,' she snorted, as if that could somehow conceal her hurt. Her shame. 'You don't need to sugar-coat it.'

'I'm not trying to sugar-coat anything,' he refuted. 'I'm trying to be sensitive. More sensitive than it seemed I was when I took you to my bed.'

She frowned. 'I seem to remember that I was the one who came to your bed.'

'Because you felt you had to.' Lukas looked disgusted, but she knew it wasn't aimed at her. 'You felt you had to have sex with me.'

'I assure you I didn't.'

Was that really what he'd thought?

'We had sex, I found out that you were a virgin, and then you told me that the most intimate you'd ever been before with anyone had been some scum who had attacked you.'

He was clearly fighting to keep his voice down, yet she knew none of his frustration was aimed at her. It was a liberating experience.

'I came to you that night because I wanted to. Because I *chose* to.'

'I'm not the man a woman like you should *choose* to give such a gift to, Oti. I don't think you fully appreciate that. This is an arrangement, not a proper marriage. The two shouldn't be confused, and sleeping together just seemed to be blurring those lines.'

'Are you saying you don't think you can trust us to share a bed without…blurring the lines?'

'I'm saying that I'm *sure* I don't trust us to.' His voice turned gravelly, and just like that her body started to melt again. And it had nothing to do with the heat.

A heavy silence settled around them, loaded with meaning and thick with desire. She opened her mouth to try to break it, but it felt as if it was impossible.

Perhaps he had a point. Every time she found herself close to him, sensations she didn't care to analyse tangled inside her, and it was getting harder and harder to push them back down. It didn't matter how ferociously she reminded herself, it seemed all too easy to forget that the agreement wasn't about *wanting* to be with the man; it was about *having* to do it.

'There's been a Hep E outbreak in the local village,' Lukas said, startling her, after a while. 'I was talking to Clay earlier and he has already been to investigate, and he found no detectable free residual chlorine in the supplies the villagers are keeping in their homes.'

'That's strange.' Oti frowned, not entirely sure why Lukas had changed the subject but trying to follow his lead, aware that Clay was their go-to water and sanitation guy. 'We always chlorinate our water before distribution. We have to. Hep E and acute watery diarrhoea can kill quickly out here. If the water isn't protected then that would likely provide a clear, active pathway for the water-borne diseases.'

'We're wondering whether contamination occurred at the tap stand, in the water container or elsewhere, and if recontamination can occur. We need some turbidimeters and photometers, as well as some chemical analysers, and then we'll head out and conduct a full investigation.'

'Great.' Oti cranked her smile up a notch, still not quite certain what was going on. 'It will be good to see the results. If there's something going wrong it's a chance to put it right and save lives.'

'I thought maybe you'd want to put together a medical team to go and vaccinate them, or treat them, or whatever Hep E needs. We could work together,' he suggested carefully. 'Albeit from different sides of the problem.'

It didn't matter how Oti tried to tell herself to rein it in, her heart started doing a little race of its own.

She didn't want to tell him that there was very little her team could do for waterborne diseases such as Hep E or acute watery diarrhoea. They could test to see if people were positive, but usually it was about preventative measures and good hygiene education.

But if Lukas wanted them to work together and maybe use that shared goal to forge a new connection and find their way back to where they'd been before, then maybe he was right.

It made sense to work alongside each other whilst forcing a little space between them on a personal level. It was logical.

The problem was...her mind and her body didn't seem to agree that *logic* was the right way to go.

CHAPTER ELEVEN

'WE'VE ISOLATED SEVERAL men and women who have tested positive for Hep E,' Oti told Lukas a few days later when he popped his head into her temporary medical tent. 'But one of them is pregnant, and another has a pregnant wife. I really need you to isolate the source before we leave, or the entire camp is going to come down with it.'

'Clay and I checked the water supplies HOP set up and they're all clean. Plus, we've done a random check on households in the camp and they've all been clean too.'

'There's definitely a source somewhere.' She frowned. 'I have too many patients suffering.'

'Which part of the camp do your patients live in?' Lukas asked. 'Maybe that will help narrow it down.'

'Yes, that might work.' Turning to her translator, Oti asked her to get the locations of their *tukuls*.

Although there was little she could do for the patients with waterborne illnesses, she'd taken the opportunity to run a children's measles drive out of the camp, and at least a thousand new displaced kids had turned up.

'Here's the list,' Oti said, thanking her colleague as she took the paper with a sketch of the area of camp and the homes. 'I'm coming with you.'

She grabbed a bagful of testing kits and instructed her staff to do the same.

As Lukas had predicted, they were clustered fairly closely together. On the downside, the tightly packed area coupled with the transmission method for the illnesses meant she was anticipating many more patients.

On the plus side, at least it meant it was likely it was something they had locally, and not a main pump or water source that had been contaminated.

'How much longer do you want to stay out here?' he asked. 'Or does your team need to get back to the main compound?'

'No, we'll be here for at least another couple of days. The number of kids who are here, and who we could vaccinate, makes it more than worthwhile. Are you and Clay heading back, then?'

She tried not to look too disappointed. It had actually proved a good idea, she and Lukas working together. Taking their various teams out of the main camp seemed to also be giving the two of them a fresh outlook, and the odd awkwardness that had settled over them ever since they'd slept together finally seemed as though it was dissipating.

'No. Even if the problem turns out to be a communal bucket which they're filling from some kind of surface water pool instead of the clean water source the charity has set up, we found one of the pumps in a deep water well on its last legs and we want to swap that out before we go back. Clay's due to be leaving in a few days so he wants to close off any jobs like this whilst he can.'

'Okay, that's good.' She fought to suppress her grin of delight. 'So we'll probably head back to camp all together the day after tomorrow.'

'Yeah, well, that's the night Clay's leaving party is scheduled, so he's pretty determined to be back by then.' Lukas laughed.

It was hopeless not to grin back at him. 'Ah, that means barbecue and beer. I can't let my team miss that or they'll never volunteer to come out with me on another away mission again.'

'Maybe we could have a drink together.'

Oti tucked her hands into her shorts pockets, just so that she didn't throw them around in delight. 'That would be nice.'

'Good.' He dipped his head as though that confirmed it. 'Then we'll have a drink at the party.'

'Okay,' she managed quietly, but he was already going, leaving her to watch his retreating rear for far longer than she knew was acceptable.

* * *

It had been a good mission, Lukas thought two days later, back at the medical camp, as he made his way across the compound to finally get a hot—hot-*ish*—shower.

Several days away and, despite the T-shirts and field washes they'd had, the work had been manual and gruelling, even without the heat to contend with. But it had been as satisfying as ever—the feeling that what he was doing was really making a difference out here.

Money was all well and good back home, but what he did here wasn't about money—it was about saving lives. Literally. And somehow it left him feeling more at peace with himself than he thought he'd ever felt.

Or maybe that was the effect Oti had on him. He couldn't deny that working alongside her had been harmonious and somehow...*right*.

But now what?

Sharing a tent with Oti the past couple of days had been taxing enough, and that was before they'd broken that invisible barrier between them. Tonight they would be back in their *tukul*—back to sharing a bed—and Lukas was forced to admit, as he crossed the compound again, he wanted her more than ever.

Perhaps he could commandeer one of the outside hammocks? It might avoid any further conflict with Oti, and he was tired enough to sleep on a clothesline, and the mosquitoes weren't a real problem during the heat of the day. It was only the evening and night when you seemed to get eaten alive.

But he'd face that problem when it arose.

Ducking into the *tukul*, he grabbed clean gear and his wash bag, then headed over to the shower block; one of the cubicles was already in use as he walked in. It didn't take him long to strip off and stand under the shower head, his foot on the manual lever that was connected to the solar-heated water collector above which would tip to rain warm water down on him.

It might not be the steaming hot power shower he had grown accustomed to, but somehow, out here, these jury-rigged systems seemed all the more blissful.

By the time he emerged from the shower, towelled off with fresh shorts on, he felt cleaner and fresher than he had in the last couple of days on the road. What was more, he felt ready to face anything, even another night in the same bed as Oti, with their backs to each other as he resisted that roaring need to turn her over and remind her just how good they had been together.

Gathering up his stuff, Lukas made to leave just as the other cubicle opened and Oti stepped out, a long, soft white shirtdress giving way to those incredible legs, her hair wrapped in a towel.

Her blue eyes widened as she saw him standing there.

'I thought you were restocking the vehicle?' It was only half an accusation.

'And I understood you were going for something to eat first,' he countered lightly, not bothering to answer the question. 'But I see you're trying to avoid me.'

'I'm not.' She tried to deny it, but suddenly Lukas decided he was sick of the game.

There was altogether too much rawness and leftover heat between them every time they found themselves alone. And the more they tried to deny themselves, the more intense it seemed to become. Which was why he found himself advancing on his new wife, revelling in that too-aware look in her eyes as he backed her up to the baked clay brick wall of the block, one arm braced against the wall behind her head and the other by his side.

Deliberately not touching her. Deliberately angling his body just enough that she could push past him if she really wanted to.

Oti didn't even attempt to.

'You missed me, didn't you?' he demanded, his voice hoarser than he'd expected.

'No.' She flushed. That deep colour which disappeared beneath the falling neckline of her top, making his hands itch to follow it. To trace her soft skin.

'Do I need to remind you what happened last time you lied?' he asked softly.

'Do I need to remind *you*?' she echoed unexpectedly, making his body pull taut.

'You do not.' His voice rasped over them. 'I remember it vividly. I've been remembering it vividly ever since it happened.'

He didn't know what it was that made him reach out to take a strand of her long, damp hair—tumbling from the towel and around her face as it was—in his fingers. He wasn't sure what made him twist it around his finger as he gazed deeply into her eyes—this woman who he now called his wife. He tugged the stray strand behind her ear as the jagged sound of her breathing seemed to echo that thing which moved within him. And he certainly couldn't explain what made him step closer to her again and lower his mouth to hers.

She melted against him instantly. The sigh she emitted was like the hottest, longest lick against the hardest part of him. Driving him crazy and making him ache all the more.

Kissing her more deeply, and angling his head for a better fit, he allowed his free hand to snake around to pull the towel from her head, dropping it to the ground before he slid his fingers into her hair.

He explored her mouth, using his lips, his tongue, his teeth. And then he explored that line over her jaw and down her neck, right round to her sensitive earlobe, and the pressure point behind.

He pressed closer and she arched against him, pressing her breasts into his chest, tight nipples grazing him even through the thin top that she wore. Enough for him to realise she wasn't wearing anything underneath it, and he lost whatever sliver of self-control he had left.

It was everything he hadn't been able to stop thinking about ever since that night. Or maybe his whole life.

With a low groan of need, Lukas brought his other hand off the wall to slide down her back, taking his time tracing her spine and over her peachy backside, before reaching for the hem of her dress and pulling it upwards. Exposing one nipple, which he proceeded to take into his mouth, drawing it against the length of his tongue.

'We shouldn't...' she rasped, though he noticed her choice of word was *shouldn't*, not *mustn't*.

'Everyone else is already at the party, unless they're working,' he murmured against the satin-soft feel of her skin, not wanting to lose contact for a second. 'They won't come in here.'

'I know,' she managed. 'We're the last...'

'So stop talking,' he growled, shifting his attention to the other side, and lavishing it with the same attention.

Her gasp of pleasure was so raw as she moaned out his name, and Lukas was lost. So lost in her heat, and her taste, and her scent. With her still arching against him, he let his hand glide down her body, taking his time to reacquaint himself with her. As though it had been years since he'd last held her, rather than a few weeks.

He let his fingers walk over every dip and every curve. Playing with her belly button and the faint swell of her belly, toying with that mouth-wateringly neat triangle before tugging aside the flimsy lace barrier and inching painfully slowly to her core.

'So wet,' he muttered, his mouth still full of her. He slipped his finger though her slick folds and revelled in the way she bumped against him already. 'So perfect.'

She moaned his name again, and it was all he could do not to wrap her legs around his hips and bury deep himself inside her. She was going to be the death of him.

He thought she probably already had been.

And then Lukas began to stroke her. Taking his time. Long, slow sweeps designed to build the tension slowly, no matter how much his hungry bride bucked against his hand.

She was breathing harder now. Choppy, ragged little sounds that made his own sex ache all the more. He couldn't remember anything ever being hotter than this. *Never.*

Carefully, he built the pace. Alternating between his mouth on her breasts, where he paid attention to one hardened nipple and then the other, to his hand between her legs. Setting the rhythm for her to follow, every breathtaking inch of her responding perfectly to his touch, he built her up, and up, until he could feel her racing towards that peak.

With a final twist of his hand that felt as though he'd been perfecting it just for this moment with *her*, Lukas sent his new bride soaring. Her head tipped back as she came apart against his hand. Shattering in his arms.

'My beautiful wife...' The words slipped out before he could bite them back, and yet he couldn't bring himself to care the way he should.

Oti was all he'd never realised he wanted, and he felt wonderfully lost in her. So lost that he almost missed the voices approaching the shower block.

'Hold still,' he commanded quietly, not letting Oti go, even as he reached behind him and pulled the shower curtain closed.

He'd been so lost in her that he hadn't even thought to do it sooner. He couldn't imagine any other woman making him this out of control. This fervent. Only her.

Only ever her.

A few moments and the newcomers would be in their respective cubicles, leaving it free for him and Oti to make their escape. It was surprising how silly and youthful he felt. It had been so long since he'd been that way. Had he ever been that way? Now he thought about it, perhaps not.

He'd begun taking care of his mother from such an early age that the usual schoolkid pranks and fun had bypassed him completely. And then he'd been so busy building up his business that there hadn't been time for frivolity.

Yet Oti made him feel fun. And youthful. It occurred to Lukas that maybe he needed a little more of this in his life.

A little more *Oti*.

A few moments later and he heard first one shower start up and then another. Carefully peering out to ensure the coast was clear, he sent his wide-eyed bride on her way back to their *tukul*, waiting a minute or so longer for the sake of appearance before following.

Oti stood hesitantly by the side of the bed, waiting for Lukas to follow her. Was their intimacy over, or was she supposed to wait for him? Her whole body still seared from his touch, and a part of her was terrified that he might have changed his mind in the moments between the shower block and their hut.

She had never, *ever* done anything that crazy before, and she'd never wanted to—though she'd never judged any of the other volunteers who might have bed—or shower—hopped over the years. It wasn't a daily occurrence, though it was common enough. They might be out here to try to do good work, but they were still red-blooded young men and women at the end of the day.

And all she wanted now was to be back in their bed. Truth be told, she'd never really wanted to leave it after their first night together. But she'd been frightened. Scared off by the intensity of her feelings for him. Now it occurred to Oti that if she wanted him she could always stop waiting for him to come to her. She could take more charge over her own destiny.

With a deep, steadying sigh, Oti pushed open the mosquito net and climbed onto the bed, her pulse racing. Moments later, Lukas crashed through the door and as he looked at her on the middle of the king-size bed she held her breath.

'Stay there,' he commanded, his voice low and rough because she affected him too much.

'I wasn't going anywhere,' she told him solemnly.

She wasn't entirely sure where that had come from; she only knew that she liked the effect it had on her husband. More than liked it.

His eyes were almost black with desire as he stripped off his shorts with ruthless efficiency, then sprang up as proud and magnificent as she remembered. Oti heard her own reverent sigh, and her mouth was suddenly parched.

She paused, a kind of wildness scrambling in her chest, and then he was climbing onto the bed next to her, scooping his arms around and flipping her flat onto her back before she realised what was happening.

This was what she'd been waiting for.

This was…

Abruptly, he stopped, and her eyes flew open. Was something wrong?

'Condom?' he managed gruffly.

'Condom?' she echoed weakly.

'Do you have any?' he demanded, leaving her blinking for a few seconds.

It took her an inordinate amount of time to process what he was saying.

'We need one.' He sounded pained. As though he could barely stop.

Oti paused, willing herself to think straight.

'I have one.' Eventually, her lips drew into a thin line. 'In the drawer of the dressing table.'

His jaw tightened.

'You keep condoms in your *tukul*? Since me, or before me?'

'It isn't *my tukul*. It's *our tukul*,' Oti pointed out, if a little breathlessly, though she couldn't say that glint of possessiveness in his tone didn't make her heart leap in triumph. 'I've never stayed in this one before you because, strangely enough, I've never been married before.'

He grunted a half acknowledgement, so she pressed on.

'But, in answer to your question, they were given to me by my boss the minute she saw you.'

'I take it that's supposed to be a compliment.' He pulled a face.

'Trust me, it is. We're medical staff. You have no idea quite how weird our sense of humour is sometimes.'

'I'm beginning to learn,' Lukas remarked drily, pulling apart the mosquito net and sliding off the bed to head to the dressing table.

'I do feel bad, though,' Oti continued as she watched him. 'The people here have so little. I feel awful about accepting from their supplies, even though I know it's for the staff too, to keep everyone safe.'

'I'll send out a hundred to replace them,' he declared, crossing back to the bed. 'A thousand. Hell, I'll even send a million, just for you to shut up and either slide that on me or give it to me to do.'

A ridiculous giggle escaped her, like some kind of schoolgirl, but Oti couldn't lament it. It felt like a side of her—the sillier side—that had been missing for so long had returned.

'I'd rather have a million tetanus shots,' she joked, as he finished pulling the net back into place, so they didn't get bitten alive.

'Done,' he ground out, flicking the condom

onto the bed with his thumb and forefinger. 'It's worth it just for this.'

'Do you have any idea how much a million tetanus shots would cost?' She laughed, tearing the wrapper and sliding out the sleeve of rubber,

Hopefully, he wouldn't see how much her hands were shaking. He was so hot, so ready, and it sent a glorious, heavy heat permeating through her entire body.

'If it means you stop worrying about using a couple of condoms from the supplies,' he managed thickly, his eyes still gratifyingly riveted on the sight of her sliding the protection over his impressive length, 'then I think I can spare the money. Didn't you know that I'm a billionaire?'

'No, I think that detail might have escaped me,' she tried for levity, but there was no escaping the need that laced her voice.

She was grateful when he took control again.

'Now stop talking and come here.'

Scooping her up, he brought her back beneath him before she'd even realised it.

'Much better,' he approved, letting his gaze roam over her, leaving a trail of fire in its wake.

And then he took his time, as if committing every dip and every curve to memory. As if he couldn't get enough of her.

Oti watched him, unable to drag her gaze away. There was an almost fierceness in his expression as he took her in. A reverence that made her feel more beautiful than she thought she'd ever felt. And then he settled between her legs again, every inch of his sex pressed into her heat, and that primitive need surged through him all over again.

'Lukas...'

'Hush, *my lady*,' he teased, his teeth grazing her neck halfway between pleasure and pain. 'Now is not the time for more words.'

As if to prove his point, he sat back on his heels, nestled between her legs. Then he reached out and simply tore her lace panties off, the raunchy sound seeming to echo in their private hut.

And finally, *finally*, he was there—where she ached for him the most. He took care lining himself up, but still he held back. She could sense it. Almost feverishly, she lifted her legs to wrap right around his body, thrilling as his blunt tip inched deeper.

'Careful,' he warned hoarsely. 'I'm not sure how long I can resist you.'

She moved her hands down his back, her fingernails skimming over his skin and making him shudder with pleasure.

'What if I don't want you to resist me?' she murmured, tilting her pelvis up.

'Oti,' he groaned. 'You deserve more...'

'Now, Lukas,' she hardly recognised the need in her own voice. 'Please...'

He slid home in an instant, a long, low sound

escaping his lips. And hers. He drew out and re-peated it. Over and over. Faster and faster. And each time she met him stroke for stroke, her legs pulling him tighter in, whilst she ran her hands down his muscular back and obliques, her palms searing everywhere she touched him.

All she could do was wrap her arms around him and cling on. Letting him drive them nearer to that exalted edge, watching it get closer and closer as her breath grew more ragged in the silent night air.

Primitive and perfect, and never-ending, until he reached down between their bodies and into her molten heat, where he performed another incredible sleight of hand trick on her core, and tumbled her into that great white void.

And as he followed her, calling out her name into her neck, Oti realised that she never wanted it to end. There was no denying the truth that was in her heart any longer.

Their wedding might have been fake, but the fact that she was falling for him was very much for real.

CHAPTER TWELVE

'DID I TELL you that I managed to call Edward on the satellite phone?'

She knew he was awake. It was hours later. After they'd slept a little, only for her to wake up in his arms and make love a second time.

The bed moved as he reached up to the frame inside the safety of the insect net and turned on the torch, the diffused light falling softly around them as he sat up and drew her in closer to him.

'He's had his surgery?'

'No, but he'll be going in for it later this week.'

'That's great news.'

'It is,' she agreed. 'He had the assessment the day after you gave us the funds. There had been a slot and I'd taken it. It's why I needed the money so urgently. He was classified as a suitable candidate, and he'll undergo the operation this week.'

'And when will you know if it worked?'

'Three months will give some indication, but nine months should give a clearer picture.'

'If he needs anything else, you come to me,

right?' Without warning, he lifted his hand and slid his fingers under her chin.

It was so unexpected, and so intimate, that Oti wanted to cry. But she refused to.

'Of course. Thank you. I just…never thought he would go through with it.'

'Why not?' Lukas cast her a curious look. 'Do you think he was afraid it wouldn't work?'

'Maybe.' She lifted her shoulders. 'Or maybe he was afraid that it *would* work.'

She wasn't surprised he eyed her strangely. Scrunching her face, she tried to find a way to explain it.

'The night my mother died she'd asked Edward to drive her to her meeting. She hated driving at night—she always said the lights dazzled her. But that night he had a work meeting, and he didn't want to drive back home to collect her, then back to the office for the meeting, only to return to pick her up. So she drove herself.'

'He blames himself,' Lukas realised. 'So why do you blame yourself for *his* accident?'

Oti didn't move. She hadn't known Lukas had been able to read that in her.

'Your father used your brother as leverage against you for years. That's more than just being a good sister. That's guilt.'

She tried to swallow, a thick ball of emotion wedged in her throat.

And then Lukas whispered to her, 'I'm on your side, no matter what, Oti.'

She choked back a sob. 'You're right,' she managed. 'Edward blamed himself for our mother's accident. And I blamed myself for Edward's. The night of his crash, that Christmas Eve, he was coming to pick me up. I'd gone to a party with some old friends—more acquaintances—but Rockman's son was there and I panicked.'

'The one who attacked you?'

'It was the first time I'd seen him since that holiday, and I was scared. I called Edward and he said he was an hour away but to hold on and he'd come and get me. The next time I saw him, he was in a coma. I believe the report that stated the accident wasn't his fault, but there's a part of me that wonders if he was maybe speeding. Just to get to me.'

'I wish you hadn't had to go through any of that, Oti,' Lukas said fiercely, after what felt like an age. 'You deserve better.'

'So did Edward. Look at him. If the operation is successful, he'll regain some use of his arms. But that's it. He'll never be back to how he was. And it will always have been my fault.'

'No, not your fault,' Lukas growled. 'It's Rockman's fault. If he hadn't assaulted you…'

There was such fury in his tone that it almost made Oti feel safe and comforted.

'So why did you marry me, Lukas? I mean, I

realise that paying some obscene sum of money was to secure my brother's company—but whose idea was it for you to marry me?'

It took a moment longer to answer, as if he wished he could give her another answer. Or maybe that was just her imagination.

'It was part of your father's price. He wanted the money, and you married off to me.'

It wasn't a surprise; she'd always known it. But still, she couldn't help but wish it was different.

Oti struggled to keep her voice even. 'Why agree? It seems like a high price.'

'It did,' he agreed, making her heart kick at his choice of the past tense. 'At the time.'

'Oh?'

'It has been a lot more...enlightening than I'd anticipated.'

She didn't need to lift her head to hear that he was smiling.

'So what do you get out of it, Lukas?'

'I get the truth.'

That did surprise her. Pulling out of his arms, she sat up so that she could look directly at him.

'What truth?'

Another pause, though he held her gaze, clearly weighing up whether or not he was finally going to share his secret. Oti didn't realise she had been holding her breath until he finally began to speak.

'I told you about my mother. I'm not going into that story again.' His voice was a study in control, and she hated it. 'But I didn't tell you about my father.'

'You told me that you didn't know who he was,' Oti said carefully.

'I lied.'

'Why?'

'It wasn't your business,' he ground out and then, looking at her again he seemed to soften, just for a moment. 'And I've never spoken about him to anyone.'

She didn't respond. What could she answer to that?

'I told you that my mother was a hotel chambermaid. Well, the man she slept with—my biological father—' he practically spat the word out '—was the son of the family who owned the hotel.'

Slowly, things began making a little more sense in Oti's head. The marriage arrangement. The man who'd so vehemently opposed it. Lukas's hostile takeover of Rockman's hotel chain.

'Your biological father is Andrew,' she breathed. 'Rockman. The Earl of Highmount.'

'He is.' Lukas could barely say the words. 'And it wasn't a one-night stand. He and my mother had a secret affair for over two years. She was deeply in love with him and, for his part, he pretended that he loved her too. But he claimed that he had to prove himself competent to run the family businesses and gain respect before he could present her to his father. My mother was stupid enough to believe him.'

She had to be careful. She could feel his pain and his rage.

'This is what your mother told you?'

Those granite-grey eyes bored into her.

'You think she lied.' There was no rancour in his tone. 'So did I, at first. But I know it to be true because I visited him when I was about twelve, when she was dying.'

'Lukas…' His name came out as a shocked whisper, but he carried on as though he hadn't heard.

'Obviously he'd married someone far more respectable by then, but my mother begged me to tell him that she was ill. She believed that he loved her deep down, but hadn't had any choice but to do what he did. So I went, and he laughed in my face.'

'That's horrible.'

'It's characteristic Rockman.' Lukas waved it aside. 'He then called my mother a multitude of names that I won't repeat, and said that her gullibility was only one of the pathetic things about her, but that he'd *kept her on his leash* because she'd known how to satisfy him in bed.'

'How cruel,' she gasped, but again he cut her off as though, now that he'd started, he needed to get his story out.

'He also had a few choice words for me, of

course. The headlines were *illegitimate*, *worthless*, *never amount to anything* and, of course, the ubiquitous *bastard.* Then he had me thrown out of his house. In fact, I think the only reason he let me in was to hear me beg for my mother, and then he could see my reaction and feed off it.'

'So he wasn't shocked by what you had to tell him? He'd known she'd fallen pregnant, and yet he'd abandoned her,' Oti said quietly. 'Both of you.'

Lukas's face twisted into something bitter and dark.

'You're not even close. He hadn't just turned his back on my mother. He'd decided the best way to keep his own image intact was to sully hers. After that first meeting with him, I decided to dig around a bit.'

'You were twelve?'

'And I was determined. My mother had never told me who he was before that day, but once I knew I went all out. It didn't take much for me to discover that her pregnancy hadn't been the secret she'd told me it had been but that his entire family had known about it. About me.'

'Yet they'd never reached out to you? Either of you?'

'No. Though I've no doubt they knew the truth, publicly they claimed he'd never touched her, and that the first time he'd ever had cause to meet her had been because he'd had to fire her from her job when he'd discovered that she had a reputation at the hotel of sleeping with the guests.'

'She didn't, though?' Oti gasped, knowing the answer but needing to ask the question all the same.

'Of course she didn't. She was besotted with him. Only him. She never even looked at another man, certainly not when I was a kid. But he also claimed that her assertion that he was the father of her unborn baby had simply been her way of getting revenge and attention, simply to wheedle a hush money payment out of his hotel chain.'

'Oh, Lukas.'

'My mother was hounded from her home, and from the village. She had no job, no husband and a baby on the way. It's an age-old story, but it's all the more devastating when the man concerned is from a powerful family, and can destroy a life—two lives—with a whisper in his friends' ears.'

'I'm so sorry. And yet she loved him all her life?'

'To the exclusion of anyone else,' he confirmed bitterly. 'Even me. Especially me. It's why she wouldn't prove that he was the father or demand a DNA test. She always claimed that if I had never been born then they would still have their *relationship*. She said he'd only done what he did because he'd had to, and that she didn't want to ruin his reputation.'

'So this is why you've never spoken about

it. Because you were ashamed.' She shook her head. 'But you have nothing to be ashamed over, Lukas. This is his wrongdoing, not yours.'

'You misunderstand,' Lukas said harshly, his eyes so hard that she felt almost crushed. 'I'm not ashamed. I never was. I'm telling you this because it was the moment I vowed to myself that I would get my revenge. The moment I vowed that I would do what my mother couldn't, and *I* would ruin his reputation.'

'Is he worth it?'

'He was determined to punish me—a twelve-year-old kid who went to see him because it was what my *dying* mother had begged me to do.'

'When he threw you out of his house.' She nodded, able to see how hurtful that must have been to an already traumatised kid.

Lukas was such a strong man that it was sometimes easy to forget he had once been a young boy. And probably a terrified one at that.

'No. Because after I left him, before I had even got back home, there were lawyers and police there threatening to send her to jail if she ever repeated her so-called lie that she had slept with him. And that I was his son. Oti, she wasn't able to get up off the couch, she was so ill, so they had broken down the door and entered, anyway. That was how much power he had then.'

'My God, Lukas...'

Oti hesitated, trying to understand. Trying to work it out.

'I can see that's how you felt as a twelve-year-old, Lukas. But why now? Why this? You're globally successful. Haven't you already won? Why not just walk away?'

'Because you can't walk away from people like the Rockmans. They're relentless. If you walk away, they take it as a sign of weakness and come after you all the harder. And when my company first started out, he used every trick he could to wipe me out.'

'He tried to wipe *you* out?'

'People said the way I took over Roc Holdings was uncharacteristically hostile.' He shrugged. 'Now you know why. But he struck the first blow. Roc Holdings was all about hotels and exclusive boutiques. They weren't interested in the tech game, or the fourth industrial revolution. But he knew who I was, and he pulled in every contact he could to try to destroy me and my business.'

'It didn't work, though,' she pointed out. 'Which surely shows how successful you are. LVW Industries is world-renowned.'

'It wasn't LVW Industries that he tried to destroy. It was my first company, one I set up as a teenager. He bankrupted me. More than that, he trampled my reputation with lies. It nearly destroyed me. And the only reason was because it was me. My company. Just because he could. He wanted me to see that he had that much power.'

'I never knew.' She shook her head, shocked. 'I still don't see how marrying me could help you,' she said dubiously.

'The reason Rockman got away with saying the things he did about my mother was because he had friends—well-connected, respected friends—who could back up what he'd said,' Lukas continued. 'Friends who could provide alibis for all the nights my mother had claimed to be with him. I vowed to make them pay too.'

'But…' she began. And then, suddenly, it all fell into place. She stared at him in horror. 'My father?'

His silence was all the confirmation she needed.

'My father was one of his friends.' She felt suddenly sick.

'Your father is the one person who could have given my mother some degree of peace before she died,' Lukas gritted out. 'If he'd only told the truth and admitted that he knew they'd been in a relationship—even if he'd simply admitted that they'd slept together.'

'Because he definitely knew?' How could she doubt it? She was under no illusions that her father had ever been honourable.

'Your father knew,' Lukas confirmed, his voice painfully raw. 'He provided Rockman with alibis for the occasions he'd been with my mother.

And then your father backed up his lies that my mother was delusional, claiming they'd never met, let alone slept together.'

'My God, you must hate him, almost as much as you hate your own father,' she breathed. 'And he knew, but he pushed me to marry you, anyway.'

'Did you really expect any better from a man who sided with his friend over his daughter, when that man's son assaulted you?'

She felt herself blanch. It was one thing knowing the truth, but it was worse hearing someone else say the words out loud.

'Maybe it wasn't…quite the way it sounds,' she managed, even as she could hear how brittle and fragile her voice was.

But the look of disgust that twisted Lukas's face terrified her.

'Are you making excuses for him?'

'No, of course not,' she denied, wondering if that was exactly what she'd been doing.

And, if so, *why?*

Already, Lukas was moving off the bed and she knew what he was about to say even before he said it; even as she scrabbled for the words to silence him, she knew she wouldn't be able to get them out.

'I should never have slept with you, especially after I assured you that I wouldn't.'

'It takes two, as they say,' she managed, though her tongue felt altogether too thick for her mouth.

How could she reverse all this? How could they get back to where they'd been a few hours before? Even just an hour ago?

'I warned you that I wasn't a good man.' Lukas was shaking his head. 'I hurt people.'

'What? No…that isn't who you are.'

'You don't know me at all,' he snarled suddenly, taking her aback. 'You don't know how bad the Rockmans are. It seems you don't even fully appreciate how duplicitous your own father is.'

'Then why don't you tell me?'

He glared at her, and Oti couldn't look away, even as she didn't dare speak.

'That man who spilled his seed into my mother claimed that I would never amount to anything, and he called me a bastard. The two things that man believes in are money and station in life. He tried to deny me both.'

'You have more money than he could ever dream of,' she told him abruptly. 'As well as respect from your peers that he has never enjoyed. And my father?'

'Your father is his last so-called friend. He is the one who allowed my mother to suffer as she did. And now he claims to have some proof of the affair my mother and Andrew Rockman were having for years. It would prove my mother truly believed he loved her, and that she wasn't sleeping with anyone else. It would clear her reputation and finally set her free, Oti.'

And himself besides, by the sound of it, though she knew better than to voice it aloud. Instead, she took a moment to absorb that.

'And you believe my father?'

'I believe that he has something. If it hadn't been for the things he said over thirty years ago, then Rockman would never have got away with painting my mother as some kind of unhinged, desperate woman. And your father may not be honourable, but he *is* self-serving. He would certainly have made sure he had something in his back pocket all these years. Otherwise Rockman would have stuck the knife in years ago.'

She paused as disbelief began to wind through her. But the more she considered it, the more she realised Lukas had a point. She'd always wondered what bonds had kept her father and the Earl of Highmount so closely tied all these years. She'd never believed they were friends in the truest sense of the word—but it made sense that her father would have kept something up his sleeve to ensure he always had the support of a family as powerful as the Rockmans.

'You can't really believe he'll tell you, though. And betray Andrew? He values the Rockman name too much.'

Lukas's expression was impassive and as hard

as she tried to get a read on him, it was proving impossible.

'It was a chance I had to take,' Lukas answered evenly, and she hated that his tone was so neutral, so controlled. That he was shutting her out from whatever was really going on. 'Your father is like a rat with a nose for the safest bet. He'll go where the power is and, these days, I hold far more of that than the Rockman family. What better way to secure his support than to marry his daughter?'

'So that's his issue.' Her voice trembled, though, and she couldn't control it. 'Not yours.'

'I should have drawn the line at the man pimping his daughter out to me. At the very least, I should never have touched you.'

'Because, of course, I had absolutely no say in the matter.' She sat up on the pallet bed, her voice as bold as she could make it.

'It's hardly the point.' Lukas didn't look impressed. 'I never should have put you in this position in the first place. I never should have come out here. This is your sanctuary.'

'I like having you here,' she murmured, but she knew he wasn't listening.

'It's done, Oti. It's over. I never should have slept with you. I told you it was a mistake.'

And then, tipping out his shoes, he pulled them on.

'I promised Clay I would check all the wells in

the surrounding villages. I should be out of camp for the rest of the mission. The marriage is over, Oti. Don't try to contact me again.'

Before she could speak, he walked away. And although she tried to follow, by the time she was dressed and outside, he was gone.

CHAPTER THIRTEEN

'You shouldn't have come here, Octavia,' Lukas ground out, not even waiting until the door to his office was closed. 'I believe I made it clear back in Sudan that whatever foolish thing we'd indulged in was over. It should never have happened.'

If he'd hoped that the month apart would make it easier to remember the terms of his agreement with her odious father, then he was beginning to realise how mistaken he'd been.

The separation had only made it even harder now to resist crossing that room and hauling her back into his arms.

Back where she belonged.

'You made that abundantly clear, yes, but I needed to see you.'

She stood across the room from him, her eyes somewhat over-bright, her face slightly pale, and evidently fighting against clenching her hands.

It made something pull tightly within his chest,

but he knew better than to allow it any airtime in his brain.

'My assistant is at your disposal. As is my driver, and the housekeeper. I can't imagine there's any requirement that they can't handle between them.'

'I'm pregnant.'

Pregnant?

Lukas froze as the word echoed around his head. It was as though the bottom had fallen out of his world and he was tumbling, hurtling through space, and there was nothing he could do to stop himself.

'You can't be,' he bit out roughly, his brain still not engaging. 'A baby was never part of the plan.'

How could it be when he'd always sworn that he would never father a child? Any baby deserved better than him.

'Then you'll have to adjust your plans.' She flashed another dazzling smile. This one didn't reach her eyes either.

'We used protection.' He was still blurting out sentences at random, as though the words were bypassing his brain.

'Not that first time.' She narrowed her eyes at him, though he at least noticed the dart of concern that flashed through them.

For a moment Lukas didn't breathe. He couldn't think straight. Come to that, he couldn't think at all. His brain felt thick, and foggy. All he could think about was old Rockman's face, right before his heart attack, when he'd imagined the day when Lukas's own son would stand in front of Lukas with the same hatred in his eyes that Lukas had shown when he was talking to Rockman.

It was why Lukas had sworn to himself that he would never have kids of his own. He'd vowed to himself that this tainted bloodline would not continue.

And now Oti was pregnant.

'You'll have to leave.'

'Leave?' She frowned at him, and he found that he hated that expression in her eyes.

As if he was somehow letting her down.

'I mean that you're free. Of me.' He bit each word out, as though that somehow made them easier to say. 'You're released from the agreement. I'll grant you a divorce now.'

'No...' she gasped, but he cut her off.

'You'll want for nothing, I'll take care of that,' he continued. 'I'll see to it that you and the baby always...'

'Our baby.'

'Pardon?' He stared at her, uncomprehending.

'*Our* baby, not *the* baby.'

His chest pulled even tighter, but Lukas was determined to ignore it.

'I'll see to it that you and the baby always have everything you need.'

'*You're* all we need.' There was a desperation to her tone now, and it threatened to unravel things within him that had been tied up—for good reason—for so many years.

'No, I'm not what anyone needs.'

'You're wrong,' Oti exclaimed. 'You're the only thing we need.'

And it worried him how much he wanted to believe her.

'This thing between us should never have happened,' he forced himself to say flatly, as though frightened to show any emotion, lest he betray himself. 'But, now that it has, the best thing you can do is put some distance between us. That baby deserves better than me for a father.'

'Why would you even think that?' she cried.

'Because I'm not a good man.' It was a fact that had never bothered him before. 'I've spent decades trying to run away from it, but I can't. Like it or not, I'm my father's own son.'

She'd crossed the room before he'd even registered that she'd moved. And her hand on his chest was threatening to make his head spin.

'You're nothing like Rockman,' she told him fiercely. 'You're a good man, Lukas. A generous man.'

'You don't know me at all,' he thundered, needing to get her hand off him, but unable to even move. Paralysed.

His brain couldn't analyse what was happening.

'Then what am I missing?' she demanded. And it seemed that the more out of control he was feeling, the more in control she was becoming. 'Because I obviously don't see the same thing that you do.'

'You see what you want to see.' He finally managed to find it in him to lift his hand and remove hers from his chest.

But, instead of resolving the issue, he found his skin was cold without her touch. And he lamented the loss.

'No, Lukas, I've finally found out the truth about you.' She offered a lopsided smile that he couldn't even begin to draw his gaze away from. 'You know, Edward has been doing a little research since his operation, reaching out to all his old friends and allies. It seems you're one of the most generous philanthropists globally, right now. You've given millions to so many charities anonymously over the years.'

'Hearsay.'

'Do you think I don't know it was you who got all those tetanus vaccines to our camp in South Sudan within a matter of weeks? No company has ever managed that before. Not to mention the other drugs, new equipment, even new vehicles you had sent through.'

'That wasn't for public consumption,' he heard himself growl out.

'I'm not *public*, Lukas. I'm your wife. And I know you're a good man.'

'I married you because I could use you, Oti. And your father.' He made himself say it, even though he knew he would hate himself for it. 'Those weren't the actions of a good man.'

'If it hadn't been you, then my father would have married me off to someone. We both know it. And I would have had no choice but to agree because I needed to try everything I could to get the surgery for Edward. You saved me.'

She spoke so softly yet with such conviction, and the words tore into him more than any harsh words she might have thrown his way.

'By chance, not by design.'

'I don't think so.' Another killer smile. 'You could have walked away, but you didn't. I think, deep down, you knew I needed you. And, somewhere along the line, I think you've fallen in love with me.'

'You're wholly mistaken,' he ground out, barely recognising his own voice. 'I have never loved you.'

'Yes, you do.'

'No, I've never loved anyone. Not even my own mother. I'm simply not capable of it.'

And this, at least, was the truth.

'You loved your foster parents. You *are* capable of it, Lukas. And you have fallen in love with me. Just as I have with you.'

And he felt as though his entire world was imploding because he'd never before known a woman like Oti, who could level him with just one of those looks of hers.

Suddenly, he wished he was a different man. A better man. The kind of man who could say the words that this incredible, huge-hearted woman wanted to hear, and mean it.

But he couldn't.

He was too damaged. Too set in his ways.

He made himself take a step away from her. Then another. He wasn't the man she thought she loved. He certainly wasn't the man he'd pretended to be in South Sudan. Or the month before that, since their wedding. Or even the five months before that, since the first moment he'd talked to her at Sedeshire Hall.

He was a man people feared, and obeyed, and envied, but he wasn't a man who people loved. That was why no one ever had.

He was as ruthless and unlovable as his own father, but then, that wasn't a surprise; they were cut from the same damaged cloth.

And no child deserved a father like him.

For a while back there, she'd thought she'd been getting through to him. She'd felt as though the wall he kept around him had begun to crumble. But then something had changed, and he'd stopped hearing her, and started to push her away again.

She couldn't put her finger on why, but now he stood apart from her, so intransigent, so distant that he might as well have been a world away, not a few feet. And something cleaved in two inside her chest. She was terribly afraid that it was her heart.

'You think you understand me, Octavia, but you don't know me at all.' It was that crisp, businesslike tone that she found she suddenly abhorred.

'I spent those weeks with you, night and day, through some pretty stressful situations, saving lives in the middle of South Sudan. I think I know you pretty well.'

'You see what you want to see,' he bit out. 'But you ignore the fact that my whole business—my entire life—has been built on revenge. On taking down the man who threw my mother and me into the gutter like used garbage the moment he found out about me.'

'You could look at it that way.' She dipped her head slowly. 'And perhaps there has been a bit of revenge in the mix, but I don't believe that is what really spurs you.'

'And how do you figure that?' he grated out. But the very fact that he was asking was enough for Oti to feel encouraged.

'I believe that what really drives you is love,

Lukas. Love for your mother. And yes, that means you hated the way your father treated her, but you've just been nursing it for so long— ever since you were twelve—that you've let it get turned upside down in your head.'

'You're wrong.'

'I don't think I am,' she pressed on earnestly, desperate to make him see it from where she stood. 'You're trapped in this suit of armour because you made it for yourself when you were a twelve-year-old, and you'd long since outgrown it and moved on, but Rockman shoved you back into it when he went after your company. Just because he could. Because that's the kind of ignoble man that he is. Believe me, Lukas, I understand. Your father is no better than mine. But that isn't who you are. I know that for a fact.'

She needed him to see the man she—and everyone back in that medical camp—saw. Probably the same man that most of his business partners and employees saw, given the way she'd seen him treat them. He knew them all by name. How many times had she heard him ask after their families, always taking the time to really stop and listen to them?

She took a chance and crossed the room again, lifting her arms to press her hands on either side of his face, forcing him to look at her.

'Lukas, you're a good man. You show this ruthless side to the world, but you sacrifice yourself for those you care about. That's how I know you love me, because you sacrificed what you wanted to go out to Sudan with me, just because you wanted to understand why I love my work so much.'

'I was curious.'

'You cared,' she corrected. 'You always care. And that's what will make you a good father. Because you'll put your child first in a way that neither of our fathers ever put us—or their other kids—first. You are your own man, Lukas. You're not Rockman. You never were.'

All she could hear was their breathing—shallow and slightly fast. He was silent for so long after that, but he didn't remove her hands. Slowly, so slowly, he dropped his forehead so that it was almost touching hers.

And then, abruptly, he straightened up again.

'You're describing the man you want me to be, Oti. An idealistic version of me. But that isn't who I am.' The agony in his voice made her heart ache. 'I'm damaged and damaging. He once said that I would ruin you, just as he ruined my mother. And he's right. How could I be anything other when I have Rockman blood running through my veins?'

'You're nothing like him.' She thumped her fist against his chest, but Lukas just grabbed it and held it still, his large hand tight around hers, and she wished he would hold on to her for ever.

'I am like him. And nowhere was it clearer than the day I married you. I didn't just choose you because I could buy off your father. I targeted you because I could manipulate you, Oti. I used you.'

'And, once again, you conveniently forget the fact that you gave me a choice. No one forced me. You dismissed my father that night and asked if I really understood what I was doing. And what of me, Lukas? Am I a bad person? I could have refused but, instead, I asked you for even more money.'

'For a noble reason,' he snorted. 'For your brother.'

'Yet I still used you.' She slid her hand from his cheek to the back of his head. 'Yet what you're saying is that I'm more than just that one action? That I deserve to be judged on more than that one less than honourable decision.'

'You're twisting things to suit your argument. Are you so blind to the truth, when I've shown you the man I really am?'

'No,' she whispered. 'You've *told* me who you *think* you are, but almost the entire time I've known you, you've shown me a completely different person. He's the man I fell in love with. And he's the man my baby needs for a father.'

'It was a lie, Oti. Everyone lies. I'm not cut out to be a husband, and I'm sure as hell not cut out

to be a father. I won't do to my child the things...
he did to me.'

'Like abandoning them, you mean?'

Lukas's head snapped back as his eyes met
hers. Black and furious again.

'I'm nothing like him. And it isn't the same
thing.'

'A moment ago, you were telling me that you
were just like him,' she pointed out. 'Now you're
saying that you're nothing like him. Which is it
to be, Lukas?'

'Does it matter?' he roared. 'You seem determined to twist my words, no matter what.'

'Only because I don't think you know the truth
for yourself. You've been in the middle of this
fight for so long now that you aren't sure whether
you're honouring your vow as a twelve-year-old
or seeing it as the good, rounded man you've become. Despite all the odds.'

'I'm trying to save you here, Oti.'

'By turning your back on your child, just as
he turned his back on you? So what's the difference between you and him?'

He looked at her as though she'd just driven a
knife through his ribs. In a way, given her experience with the Earl, she felt as though she might
have done just that.

But she was battling for her baby. For *their*
baby. And if she had to shock him into realising
the truth, then she was prepared to do it.

'The difference—' his fury practically simmered '—is that I'm sending you away to protect you.'

'How does that protect me?' she demanded.

'Because when I take Rockman down for good, when I prove how he lied all these years, he's going to want revenge, Oti. But I'm relatively protected. There's very little the world doesn't already know about me. So who do you think he'll go after?'

'So you think sending me away will keep me safe?'

'Because it will. But I'll still provide for you financially—whatever you both need, it'll be yours. And I will never, *never* deny my child.'

'Don't be an Icarus,' she begged, 'flying too close to the sun.'

'This isn't about ambition, Oti. This is about revenge. I want to take the man down. He *deserves* to be destroyed.'

'I understand,' she said quietly, her heart and soul aching for him. For the man he was now, but especially for the little boy he'd been back then. 'Believe me, I know. But you know if you do that you'll end up destroying yourself too.'

'I know. And that's why I'm divorcing you.' He moved to the door, turning back only once as he stood, holding it open for her. And the look he shot her was nothing short of bleak. 'I need you to leave.'

'But I love you,' she pleaded. As if that could somehow solve everything.

She thought he hesitated for a brief moment, as though a part of him desperately wanted to believe her but he couldn't quite let himself. And then he went cold again, his expression almost forbidding.

'Then, believe me, Oti, you're the only one who ever has. Now, leave.'

CHAPTER FOURTEEN

OTI STARED OUTSIDE. The rain lashed against the windows, the wind screaming around the building. A perfect storm to match the one howling inside her, just as it had been for the last two days, since Lukas had thrown her out of his office.

But she was going to let it roar and rage for as long as it took, because it couldn't go on for ever. And when it eventually blew itself out, she would pick up the pieces of her shattered heart and she would move on, just as she'd told Lukas he needed to do where his father was concerned, and she would make a life for herself, and this precious baby she carried inside her.

Lukas's baby.

And no matter how much he'd hurt her—because she had sobbed for hours and hours when he'd sent her away—or how much she'd tried to tell herself that she was better off without him, she couldn't bring herself to hate him.

He had given her this inestimable gift, which meant she could never regret a moment of their time together. No matter that she was humbled by it, whilst he was immune to it.

The knock at the door caught her off guard.

Unfolding herself from the sofa, she moved across the room. She knew it was him even as her hand reached for the handle.

Hesitating for a fraction of a second, she closed her fingers around the cold metal and carefully opened the door to see him braced against her door frame. A bleak expression that she didn't think she'd ever seen before clouded his face.

It was a small comfort that he looked as drawn and drained as she felt. Perhaps worse.

He didn't move at first, and she didn't speak. And then, without waiting for an invitation, he moved past her into her apartment. Belatedly, she realised that she had stepped aside enough to allow it, her guard down.

A mistake she wouldn't make again.

Those granite-grey eyes seemed to root her to the spot, made her skin pull tight.

Jerking herself back to the moment, she would never know how she managed to galvanise her legs into action, carrying her away from him as though mere physical distance could somehow protect her heart.

'Did you mean it when you said you love me?' he demanded.

She drew in a deep breath. 'I love the man I saw in Sudan. The one who was full of life and fun. Not this version of you, mired in the past and weighed down by revenge that is, frankly, beneath you.'

It wasn't a complete answer, yet Lukas nodded, as though this was enough for him.

'I contacted your brother the other day, Oti.'

The heavy door slipped from her fingers as she turned to look at Lukas. Neither of them heard the loud bang as it slammed closed in the breeze.

'You spoke to Edward?'

'I did. I asked him how he was doing after his operation, and then I told him that he was getting his company back.'

'You're returning Sedeshire International to him?'

She wanted to ask more. She needed to understand. But her entire body felt numb. Paralysed. Her tongue was glued to the roof of her mouth, as if she'd just eaten one of her brother's infamous peanut butter sandwiches.

'It was his company, his baby. Edward's hard work built it into what it was. And he only lost it all because the board lost faith in him after the accident. And because your father is too weak and incompetent to make a business decision if it killed him.'

'Sedeshire International *was* Edward's baby. Just like LVW Industries is yours,' she managed.

'Not any more.' Lukas shocked her by shaking his head. 'Not now I know what it's like to be expecting a different kind of baby. *Our* baby.'

Her heart stuttered and leapt. He'd said '*our* baby.'

'What about taking down the Rockman family?'

'I think Edward can do that all by himself. Turns out your brother may hate them even more than I do.'

He didn't add that it was because of Louis Rockman attacking her. He didn't need to.

'He does,' she agreed quietly. 'You know, in many ways we are the same, you and I.'

'You are the daughter of an earl. And I am the son of a single, unwed mother. I hardly think that makes us the same.'

'We both had mothers who loved bad men, oblivious to their faults. Mothers who couldn't see the truth even though it was staring them in the face. The only difference was that you had to see your mother worship your father from afar, whilst I had to watch mine do it right before my eyes.'

There was sheer torment in Lukas's eyes just then. But he simply pulled his jaw taut, took a breath and then released it.

'In any case, I should go.'

'So…that is what you came here to say?' Oti asked in disbelief.

'It is.'

'That is *all* you came here to say? Nothing more?'

'Nothing more. I just wanted to tell you that you were right,' Lukas acknowledged with a rueful upturn of his mouth. 'And to thank you.'

'To thank me?'

'For showing me a different way to be. For seeing past the demons in me, to the good, I guess. If someone as gentle and good as you can love even a little bit of me, it gives me hope.'

'Hope?' she echoed again.

'Yes.' He cast her an odd look. 'Anyway, I've had an account set up in your name. Tell me how much you need for you, and for our baby. It will be in there.'

'I don't want your money, Lukas,' she choked out. 'I don't want anything from you.'

She couldn't have said what that expression was that twisted his features. Or perhaps it was more that she didn't want to identify it. It made his words echo too loudly around her head.

That if she loved him, then she was the only one who ever had.

It tore her up, and yet simultaneously made her more determined.

His situation was heartbreaking, and it made his rejection of her all the more understandable, even if it didn't make it hurt any less. But she refused to allow him to throw it all away, just because he didn't understand it.

She'd helped him see a better way once. Surely she could do it again.

'Is that all you really came here to say?' she challenged. 'You're going to throw away the fact that I love you? The fact that you love me?'

'I don't even know what love is, Oti. I wish I did. I wish I was that kind of man. But you wouldn't want whatever half-baked idea of love that I could offer.'

'You know how to love, as determined as you might be to pretend otherwise.'

'And you're determined to ignore what's right in front of your face,' he growled, misery etched into his ridiculously handsome face, which looked all the more beautiful to her right at that moment.

'You do,' she urged him softly. 'You've already shown me you do, several times. You just can't bring yourself to see it. But I can help you…if you'll let me.'

She watched him hesitate, those grey eyes shot through with uncertainty, but also with a kind of longing that pulled at her heart.

She had him. For better or worse, she had him. Relief and triumph punched through her.

'I want you, Oti, with every fibre of my being,' he told her fiercely. 'And I don't believe that feeling will ever diminish. More than that, I don't want it to. But I also want what's best for you and for our baby, and I don't believe that's me.'

Subconsciously, his eyes dropped to her belly, and she took the opportunity to close the gap between them. Then, taking his large hands in her own, she placed them over her stomach.

'It is what's best for us,' she confirmed softly. 'And what you've just described is the very definition of love.'

It felt as though her heart was lodged somewhere in the vicinity of her throat.

'You love me, Lukas, and I love you. It really is as simple as that.'

'I still don't know what that is,' he told her, but this time his voice was softer. Awed. 'I don't know if I can be what you need.'

'You can,' she assured him. 'I know you can make me happy, Lukas.'

'If you truly believe that, then I'll willingly spend my whole life trying to make it so.'

She patted his hand where it still lay over her belly.

'What's more, you will make our baby happy.'

He watched her for a moment, speechless. And then, at long last, he kissed her.

It poured through her, wild, and hot, and perfect. As if she—and their baby—were the only things that mattered to him.

It said all the things that he couldn't yet say,

and it spoke of for ever. And as Oti wrapped her arms around his neck and kissed him back, she decided happily that was more than enough to be getting on with.

EPILOGUE

MAXIMILIAN CHARLES WOODS roared into the world seven months later. A gloriously bawling eight-pound bundle who sounded as fiercely determined as his father had always been.

He wrapped his fingers around his father's large thumb and squeezed mightily, and Lukas was besotted.

So was Edward, who had wheeled himself to the hospital as soon as Lukas had called him. He had taken his young nephew in his arms and held him in the way he would never have believed possible nine months earlier.

And later that night, when Lukas and Oti were alone again, their cherished baby in their arms, Lukas lifted his eyes to his wife, those granite-grey depths spilling over with emotion.

'I never knew my heart could feel so full,' he told her huskily.

'You love us.' She nodded solemnly.

'I love you,' he confirmed, as he had so many times before. It had come hesitantly at first, but then, as if that first time was all he'd needed, she'd heard it again and again.

More than that, he had shown her he loved her, wholly and thoroughly, each and every day. He'd applied himself to it with the same drive and focus that he applied to everything that he did.

He had turned out to be an even better husband than Octavia had dreamed, and already he had proved that he would never be the kind of father that his, or hers, had been.

Max would never want for love, and he was going to have the role model that Lukas had never had. She had known that Lukas would make her happy, but she hadn't appreciated just how much he would make her heart swell.

'I never dreamed that I could have a wife. A family,' he marvelled. 'People who want me for *me*. Not for the billionaire, or the knighthood. Yet you looked past all that. You looked past the broken man inside, empty and unfulfilled, and you saw who I could be.'

'Only after I'd dragged you halfway around the world to live in a *tukul*. I saw the version of you that no one else got to see.'

'And about a million mosquitoes.' He laughed, leaning down to press his lips to her forehead. 'But I want to be that version of myself. For you. With you. And with our son. I couldn't want for anything more.'

'Don't be too sure,' she told him, her voice

thick with love. 'I have plans for a whole team of little Woods children running around.'

And Oti was true to her word.

Two years later, they added a daughter to their family, who came out less fiercely than her brother, but with a grip on life—and her father's thumb—that was equally strong. And, two years after that, twins, a girl and a boy.

They were sitting in the snug at Sedeshire Hall, having settled the last of their brood to sleep, and having bid farewell to both Edward, who lived independently in the gatehouse, and her father, who had mellowed considerably at the arrival of his grandchildren and now lived in his own apartment in the north wing.

'He wants to be a part of Max's life.' Oti had bitten her lip as she'd told Lukas, a few months after their eldest son's birth. 'He asked for a second chance, but I don't know if it's a good idea.'

'What would have happened if you hadn't given me a second chance?' Lukas had replied softly. 'I would have stayed bitter and lost, seeking revenge and destroying myself in the process.'

'But now...?' she had prompted gently.

'Now I'm happy, contented. I'm fulfilled. Driven by the love of a family who I love, rather than driven by revenge for a man who I don't even waste a thought on any more. Just as you told me would happen.'

'So I should give him a second chance?'

'That's your decision.' He'd laughed, dropping a kiss onto her lips. First one side, then the other, as she'd sighed and silently prayed their baby son would give them an hour of quiet to themselves. 'But I will support any decision you make.'

As he had done. And in all the years since. They had supported each other, and together they'd set up the Woods Foundation, offering not just a financial boost to any number of charities, but advice, experience and services. From setting up cold storage facilities to store vaccines for medical camps or desalination plants providing fresh water to desert communities, to local community projects like planting trees in parks, and setting up centres for children who acted as carers for their parents.

But as they snuggled together, their four children miraculously all asleep at the same time, Oti turned her face up to her husband's.

'You really have made me happy,' she whispered.

'I told you that I would,' he deadpanned, lowering his head to claim her mouth with his before she could object. A deep, stirring kiss that made promises for the rest of the night. Five years after their first kiss at the altar, he still had the same power to set her heart thumping and leave her feverish for more.

Even so, she managed to punch his chest lightly.

'I think you'll find it was me who said that you would,' she managed when they finally surfaced.

'Are you quite sure? I seem to remember it differently.'

'You really are the most aggravating man.' She laughed.

'Yes, I think that was what you were lamenting this morning into the pillow, when your legs were draped over my shoulders.'

'You're impossible.' Oti batted him as he offered a wicked smile that shot straight through her body.

'I am,' he agreed. 'And I love you, Lady Octavia Woods, just as I love our family. My only goal is to make you the happiest family alive. It always will be.'

And then he lowered his mouth to hers and set about proving it. Right until the stars began to twinkle in the inky blue sky. Then again, just before the sunrise began to turn the sky a welcoming yellow, and the first of the Woods brood began to roar at the top of his lungs.

* * * * *